Homecoming Queen

Just then the Laundromat lights came back on. As Melissa's eyes adjusted to the returning light, she saw what had fallen out of the dryer.

It was Betsy, hanging halfway out of the machine.

Her eyes were closed and she wasn't moving.

At first Melissa thought it was another joke. Laurel and Betsy had probably noticed that she had left her books behind. Figuring she'd return to get them, they'd decided to get back at her.

But then she saw the note pinned to the front of Betsy's blouse. There was only one sentence: THE ONLY GOOD QUEEN IS A DEAD QUEEN.

Look out for:

Double Date
Sinclair Smith

Pool Party
Linda Cargill

Also available in the Point Horror Unleashed series:

Transformer
Philip Gross

Blood Sinister
Celia Rees

The Carver
Jenny Jones

At Gehenna's Door
Peter Beere

Point Horror

HOMECOMING QUEEN

JOHN HALL

SCHOLASTIC

Thanks once again to my good friend,
Jennifer Sawyer, for listening while I plotted.

Special thanks also to my editor, Ann Reit, for giving me
a chance and asking me to write this story.

Scholastic Children's Books,
Commonwealth House, 1-19 New Oxford Street, London WC1A 1NU

New York ~Toronto ~ Sydney ~ Auckland

First published in the US by Scholastic Inc., 1996
First published in the UK by Scholastic Ltd, 1997

Copyright © John Scognamiglio, 1996

ISBN 0 590 19639 1

Printed by Cox & Wyman Ltd, Reading, Berks.

To Vincent
The Best Brother in the World

Chapter 1

"Are your eyes closed, Izzy?" seventeen-year-old Melissa Brady asked through her bedroom door.

"They're closed," Izzy answered.

"Yours, too, Celeste?"

"Closed." Celeste sighed. "Come on, Melissa. Open the door. We're going to be late for class."

"Chill out, Celeste," Melissa said. "We're seniors now. We don't have to be in homeroom until the second bell rings."

"What's the big secret?" Celeste demanded. "I know we didn't see each other all summer, but we would have connected at school."

The big secret is the new me, Melissa thought as she stared across the room at her image in the mirror over her dresser. She still couldn't believe what she was seeing. Gone was the girl who used to wear glasses, had braces on her teeth, and still hadn't outgrown her last five pounds of baby fat. Standing in her place was a new Melissa Brady, complete with contact lenses, no braces, and a great summer tan. Plus, the baby fat was gone!

"Okay, okay," Melissa said, opening the door. "The suspense is over. You can take a look."

Izzy and Celeste opened their eyes at the same time. Both gasped in surprise when they saw Melissa.

"Melissa, is that really you?" Celeste asked.

"You look great!" Izzy exclaimed, rushing into the bedroom and giving Melissa a quick hug. "What happened over the summer? I thought you were going to work as a camp counselor."

"I did," Melissa said.

"But you're so thin!" Celeste exclaimed.

"Running after hyperactive eight-year-olds will do that to you. And the food was awful." Melissa made a face. "Yuck! It made Miss Hojer's cafeteria specials look like gourmet cuisine."

"Other than the food, how was it?" Izzy asked.

"I had a blast!"

"Meet any guys?" Izzy asked.

"I did meet someone," Melissa confessed.

"There was a boys' camp across the lake."

"Spill!" Izzy exclaimed, flopping down on Melissa's bed. "I want *all* the details!"

Melissa sat at the foot of her bed. "There's not much to tell," she admitted. "His name was Mike. We went canoeing a few times, swimming, hiking. And we had a picnic one afternoon."

"Get to the good stuff," Izzy urged. "Any lip action?"

Melissa blushed. "We kissed once or twice."

"Are you still seeing him?" Celeste asked.

Melissa shook her head. "He lives across the country."

Celeste gave Melissa a sympathetic smile. "You broke up."

"We weren't really dating," Melissa explained. "We were only friends. But we are going to keep in touch and write each other."

"I love what you've done with your hair," Izzy raved. "Did you dye it?"

"It's from the sun," Melissa said, running a hand through her shoulder-length chestnut-brown hair shot with strands of gold. "Like it?"

Izzy nodded her head. "The color is wild. I wish my hair looked that way."

"You don't exactly have much to work

with," Melissa pointed out, eyeing Izzy's very short buzz cut.

Izzy brushed the palm of her hand over the spiked top of her brunette head. "It'll grow back."

"In about six months!" Celeste exclaimed. "What are you going to do when it's time to take graduation pictures?"

Izzy shrugged her shoulders. "Smile and say cheese. What else?"

Melissa laughed. Sometimes she wished she had the courage to be as independent and outrageous as Izzy. She didn't care what anyone thought about her. Or the way she dressed. Izzy didn't adhere to current fashions but created her own, mixing and matching whatever she liked. Izzy loved vintage clothes and was constantly going to yard sales and flea markets looking for things to add to her wardrobe. Today she was wearing a tiny black miniskirt with a hot-pink crocheted top and mod boots, straight out of the sixties.

Celeste, on the other hand, was ultraconservative. As always, she was wearing a cotton blouse, jeans, and penny loafers. Her dark brown hair was pulled back in a ponytail and she didn't have any makeup on. Unlike Izzy, Celeste never did anything that would draw attention to herself. Some of their classmates thought she was boring, but Melissa knew that beneath Celeste's serious exterior was a warm and friendly person. The same with Izzy. She might look like a wild party animal, but she wasn't.

Melissa knew she was lucky to have Izzy Jacobs and Celeste DiPaglia as her best friends. She'd never forget the way they'd showed her the ropes when she arrived at Westdale High last winter. It had been strange starting a new school in the middle of the year, but from her first day Izzy and Celeste had been there to help her fit in.

Melissa hugged Izzy and then Celeste. "I really missed you guys."

"We missed you," Izzy said. "When I wasn't working at the mall I was stuck baby-sitting my bratty niece."

Melissa began gathering her backpack and car keys. "How was your summer, Celeste?"

Celeste shrugged. "The same as it's been the last three years. I took an advanced class in summer school. Precalculus."

"Don't you hate always having your nose buried in a book?" Izzy asked.

"It's not like I have a choice," Celeste said. "If I want to get into a good college, I've got to to earn a scholarship."

Suddenly Melissa felt guilty for having had

such a fun summer. She knew it was tough for Celeste's family to make ends meet. Her father worked two jobs and her mother cleaned houses. Celeste's parents could never afford to pay college tuition, which was why Celeste was so determined to win a scholarship.

"Don't worry," Melissa said. "I'm sure so many colleges are going to offer you scholarships, you won't know which one to choose."

Celeste gave Melissa a smile. "Thanks."

"So what happened to your braces and glasses?" Izzy asked.

"I made trips to the dentist and the eye doctor last week," Melissa said.

"We'd better go," Celeste interrupted, glancing at her watch, "or we're going to be late."

"Wouldn't want to spoil your perfect attendance record," Izzy teased, bouncing off Melissa's bed and following after Celeste.

Tossing her backpack over one shoulder, Melissa hurried after Izzy and Celeste, smiling as she heard them bickering.

It was good to be home.

"Can you believe we've got *Jabrowski* for homeroom?" Izzy groaned as they walked across the student parking lot. "He makes everyone sit in alphabetical order and doesn't allow any talking."

"Besides homeroom, how many classes do we have together?" Celeste asked as they climbed up the faded redbrick steps of Westdale High. "I'm taking A.P. English, A.P. History. . . ."

"Celeste!" Izzy wailed. "Why are you taking such a heavy-duty load? It's our senior year!"

"Colleges are very impressed by students who take advanced classes," Celeste said.

"I've waited three years to be a senior," Izzy said as they maneuvered their way through the crowded hallways. "I plan on coasting this year."

"Then I guess the only time we'll see each other — besides homeroom, that is — is at lunch," Celeste said as they walked up the stairs to the second floor and headed for their lockers — the same ones they'd had since they'd come to Westdale High. "What's your schedule like, Melissa?"

"I tried to take a mix," Melissa said as she worked the combination of her lock.

"Don't look now, Melissa," Izzy whispered as she opened her locker and dumped her books inside, "but someone is checking you out."

"Who?"

"Who would you like it to be?" Izzy asked.

"Seth Powell?"

"Maybe . . ."

"Izzy!"

"Okay, okay!" Izzy admitted. "He's looking at you."

Melissa took a quick peek at herself in the mirror hanging on the inside of her locker. Her makeup was perfect; hair all in place. She started to turn around, but Izzy stopped her. "Don't look at him!"

"Why not?"

"Jocks like Seth Powell think they can smile at any girl they want and she'll come running."

"My feet are already moving!" Melissa said, laughing.

"Take my advice and play hard to get," Izzy said, closing her locker. "It'll make him more interested if he thinks you're unattainable."

Celeste nodded her head knowingly. "Izzy's right. Guys always want what they can't have."

The second bell rang and Melissa followed Izzy and Celeste to homeroom. It was hard not looking over her shoulder at Seth, but she took Izzy and Celeste's advice and pretended not to notice him.

Homeroom was a madhouse. A radio was blaring and the noise level was high as clusters of students who hadn't seen each other all summer talked nonstop.

"Guess Mr. Jabrowski is running late," Celeste said as they slipped into three desks by the windows.

"Don't look now, but here comes the Gruesome Twosome," Izzy muttered under her breath.

Melissa looked across the classroom, catching sight of Laurel Schaeffer and Betsy Sullivan. As usual, they were joined at the hip. Melissa didn't say anything. She knew Izzy would be appalled if she told her she wished she could be friends with Laurel and Betsy.

Laurel, a tall blonde, and Betsy, a tiny redhead, were the two most popular girls at Westdale High. Besides being cheerleaders, they were on all the committees that mattered, went to the best parties, and always wore the latest fashions.

Laurel and Betsy were outgoing and bubbly, and Melissa wanted to be the same way. If there was one thing she hated about herself, it was her shyness. Because she was always afraid of what other people would think of her, Melissa usually made an effort not to be noticed. Instead, she blended into the background, watching what was going on around her before becoming involved.

But Melissa didn't want to be a part of the background anymore. This year she wanted to make things happen and know what it was like to be the center of attention. Like Laurel and Betsy.

Trailing behind Laurel and Betsy were Seth Powell and Zach Kincaid. Betsy and Zach had been going steady since they were sophomores, but Melissa knew Laurel and Seth had only started dating last semester.

"Are Seth and Laurel still an item?" she whispered in Izzy's ear.

Izzy followed Melissa's gaze. "I don't know," she answered. "I'll find out and get back to you at lunch."

Melissa tried to keep her eyes off Seth, but was unable to. He was *so* cute! With his blond hair and baby-blue eyes, he looked like a California beach boy heading for the surf. Melissa couldn't help having a secret crush on him, especially after he'd been nice enough to help her find a class when she'd needed directions last spring.

Laurel, Betsy, Seth, and Zach headed for four desks in the back of the classroom. As Seth passed by Melissa's desk, he gave her a smile.

Before Melissa could decide if she should smile back, a silence fell over the classroom.

Turning around in her seat, Melissa saw the imposing figure of Mr. Jabrowski in the doorway. He walked over to the desk in front of the classroom and dropped his briefcase.

"Due to car trouble, I was unavoidably detained," he began. "We won't have time for seat assignments today, but we will tomorrow."

"Uh-oh," Izzy whispered into Melissa's ear. "Laurel's sending you the evil eye. Guess she saw Seth smile at you." Izzy threw her hands up in front of her face. "I'm melting!" she cried. "Melting!"

Melissa playfully swatted Izzy's arm and dared a look in Laurel's direction. She immediately wished she hadn't when she saw Laurel glaring at her.

Melissa smiled at Laurel, but Laurel didn't smile back. Instead, she leaned over to Betsy and whispered in her ear. Betsy glanced at Melissa and then giggled.

Uncomfortable, Melissa turned her back on Laurel and Betsy and listened to the announcement Mr. Jabrowski was making.

"For the first time in twenty-five years, Westdale High will be having a Homecoming Weekend next month. That will include the tradition of electing a Homecoming king and queen. Nominations will be taken for a ballot this week, and then there'll be three weeks of campaigning. Anyone who's interested in nominating someone for Homecoming king or queen will have the chance to do so at this afternoon's assembly."

An excited buzz traveled throughout the classroom, followed by shouts of disbelief and hushed whispers. Melissa looked around in confusion. What was going on?

As she glanced around the classroom, Melissa noticed something else.

Something strange. Was it fear?

Chapter 2

"It's nice to know Miss Hojer's cooking is still the same," Izzy said, taking the seat between Melissa and Celeste and plopping down her lunch tray.

"What *is* that?" Celeste asked, warily sniffing the steaming brown mass on Izzy's tray.

"It's supposed to be turkey, but I'm not sure." Izzy glanced at the sandwich Melissa was unwrapping. "Is that tuna fish?"

Melissa paused in the middle of taking a bite. "Yes, it is."

Izzy looked at the sandwich suspiciously. "It's not Tasty Tuna, is it?"

"My mom doesn't buy Tasty Tuna. It's another brand."

Izzy gave a sigh of relief. "Good. I'm boycotting Tasty Tuna and you should, too. Did you know they're killing dolphins with their nets?"

Melissa shook her head. "Thanks for the info."

"Hey, Izzy, any news on Seth and Laurel?" Celeste asked eagerly.

Izzy gave Celeste a smug smile, digging into her mashed potatoes. "Wouldn't you like to know!"

"Izzy!" Melissa wailed. "I've been waiting all morning for this!"

"They're splitsville!" Izzy announced.

"Who dumped who?" Celeste asked.

"Seth dumped Laurel over Labor Day weekend," Izzy said around a mouthful of turkey.

"If they're not dating anymore, why would she care if Seth was interested in me?" Melissa asked.

Izzy shrugged her shoulders. "You're asking me?"

Melissa took another bite of her sandwich. "Can you tell me something else?"

Izzy nodded her head. "Sure."

"What's the deal with Homecoming queen?"

"What do you mean?" Celeste asked.

"Some kids in homeroom acted strangely after Mr. Jabrowski made his announcement," Melissa explained.

"They're probably afraid Brenda Sheldon's ghost is going to haunt them," Izzy snickered.

Melissa gave Izzy a puzzled look. "Who's Brenda Sheldon?"

"What do you mean, 'Who's Brenda Sheldon?' Everyone knows who Brenda Sheldon is."

"I don't."

Izzy slapped herself on the forehead. "That's right! You *don't* know who she is. You didn't grow up in Westdale."

"So are you going to fill me in?"

"Let me tell it," Celeste volunteered, pushing away her potato chips and moving her chair closer to Melissa's. "Twenty-five years ago," Celeste began, "Brenda Sheldon was crowned Westdale High's Homecoming queen. Everyone knew she was going to be queen because everyone liked her and had voted for her. She wore a white gown to the Homecoming dance and when she was crowned, she looked like a princess."

"Sounds wonderful," Melissa said.

Celeste nodded her head. "It was. The dance lasted for hours and when it was finally over, all Brenda wanted to do was go home. But her boyfriend, Jake Corsi, who was Westdale's star quarterback, wanted to party a little longer with the rest of the Homecoming court. They convinced Brenda to drive out with them to Blue Willow Woods, telling her they couldn't party without their queen. Even though Brenda had a curfew and knew she had to be home by midnight, she decided to tag along with her friends."

"Big mistake," Izzy added.

Suddenly Melissa didn't want to hear what had happened to Brenda Sheldon. She knew it wouldn't be good.

"By this time it had started to rain," Celeste continued. "The streets were slick and the road they were taking to Blue Willow Woods had lots of curves. The brakes on Jake's car weren't very good and needed to be replaced. He'd planned on doing it the day before but didn't get a chance."

"Mistake number two," Izzy said.

Celeste ignored Izzy's comment. "Jake was driving too fast. He was speeding because he wanted to be the first to get to Blue Willow Woods. He was also drinking. One of his friends had brought along a case of beer."

Drinking and driving. Melissa knew the two were a deadly combination.

"The accident happened when Jake swerved around the first curve in the road," Celeste said. "Instead of staying in his lane, he veered into the opposite lane . . . and into the path of a truck headed straight for them."

Melissa gasped. She could imagine the cold glare of oncoming headlights in the darkness of night. The loud blare of the truck's horn.

The screams of terror.

"Jake wasn't able to stop his car," Celeste whispered. "They crashed head-on. No one was wearing a seat belt and everyone in the car died, including Brenda."

"You forgot to mention one little thing," Izzy said. She slid a finger across her throat. "Brenda was decapitated."

"Eew! Gross!" Melissa cried.

Celeste sighed. "Izzy, that's not true. You've been listening to too many ghost stories."

"How do you know it's not true?" Izzy demanded. "Were you there?"

"No, but I've read some of the old newspaper clippings in the school library. None of them mention Brenda's head being cut off."

Izzy bit into a chocolate-chip cookie. "Must have been edited out."

Celeste turned back to Melissa. "In memory of the five students who were killed, Westdale High decided to no longer have Homecoming. The school felt that the true spirit of Homecoming had been lost and students only wanted an excuse to drink and party. Plus, not having Homecoming was a way of honoring the dead."

"The spooky thing," Izzy added, lowering her voice, "is that some people swear they've seen Brenda's ghost walking through Blue Willow Woods in her bloody white dress. They say she's trying to find her way back to Westdale High so she can reclaim the crown and scepter she left behind."

Goose bumps rose over Melissa's arms. "If the last Homecoming was so horrible, why is Westdale High starting up the tradition again?"

Izzy gazed around the cafeteria. "Have you taken a look at this place lately? It's a dump. The school's falling to pieces and needs major repairs. It also needs money to buy new equipment and supplies. Having alumni come back to Westdale is a good way to get donations."

"Guess I know everything there is to know about Brenda Sheldon," Melissa said. "I'm almost sorry I asked."

"Asked what?" a voice said.

Melissa recognized the voice but wasn't sure if she was hearing correctly. She looked across the table and saw Seth Powell standing with his lunch tray.

"It's Melissa, right?"

Melissa nodded her head. He knew her name! She couldn't believe it. Seth Powell, whom she'd been dreaming about all last semester, knew her name!

Seth pointed to the empty chair across from Melissa. "Is this seat taken?"

"It's all yours."

"Thanks." He sat down and bit into his hamburger. "What are you guys talking about?"

"Brenda Sheldon," Izzy stated.

"Is she still looking for her head?" Seth asked, squeezing some ketchup over his French fries.

Izzy stuck her tongue out at Celeste. "Told you so."

"How was your summer?" Seth asked Melissa.

"Fine. Yours?"

"Okay. You look great. I almost didn't recognize you in homeroom."

Melissa blushed. "Thanks."

"Won't Laurel mind that you're having lunch with us?" Izzy asked, snatching a French fry off Seth's plate.

"Why would she mind?"

"There's a rumor going around that you and Laurel broke up at the end of the summer, but this morning in homeroom you looked like you were her shadow."

"Just because I followed her into class and had to sit next to her because there were no other seats?"

"Then it's over between the two of you?"

Izzy asked. "You're free and clear?"

Seth looked directly at Melissa. "Yep."

Butterflies were crashing around in Melissa's stomach. She couldn't believe this was happening. Finally she managed to find her voice. "How have your classes been going?" she asked.

"So far, so good." Seth took a sip of his vanilla shake. "This afternoon is going to be a killer, though. I've got Ms. Kazmier for anatomy."

"Me, too!" Melissa exclaimed.

Seth gave Melissa a smile before finishing off the last bite of his hamburger. "Guess I'll see you in class, then. Maybe we'll be lab partners." He checked the time on his watch. "Gotta run or else I'm going to be late for gym." He snatched his books off the table and tucked them under one arm. "See you later."

"Later," Melissa said, watching Seth race out of the cafeteria. When she turned back around in her seat she found Izzy and Celeste staring at her with huge grins on their faces.

"Looks like Melissa might be getting a boyfriend this year," Izzy said. She picked up her lunch tray and headed for the nearest trash can. "What do you think, Celeste?"

"I think you're right, Izzy," Celeste agreed.

"Get a grip," Melissa said, following after

them. A guy like Seth interested in *her*, after having dated a girl like Laurel? "You're jumping to conclusions."

"We are not," Izzy said. "Seth likes you, Mel. Why won't you believe it?"

Because it seems almost too good to be true, Melissa thought.

"Uh-oh, here comes trouble," Izzy muttered under her breath.

Melissa looked past Izzy and saw Laurel and Betsy headed in their direction. Instantly the butterflies in her stomach died, replaced by a feeling of dread.

"Hi, Melissa," Laurel said with a smile. "I love your new look. Isn't it fabulous, Betsy?"

"Absolutely," Betsy agreed.

Even though Laurel and Betsy were both smiling and being nice, Melissa felt uncomfortable. Unable to look them in the eye, she stared down at the floor. "Thanks."

"Can I give you some advice, Melissa?" Laurel said, her voice still sugary sweet. "It's not smart going after another girl's boyfriend."

Melissa was confused and she looked up at Laurel. "What are you talking about?"

"Seth."

"But he's your *ex*-boyfriend," Melissa said. "He broke up with you over the summer."

Laurel shook her head. "Our breakup is only

temporary. We'll be getting back together. Soon."

"That wasn't what he told Melissa," Izzy interjected smugly.

"Get real!" Laurel exclaimed, all pretense of friendliness gone. "Why would Seth be interested in Melissa? She may look a little different on the outside, but inside she's still the same."

"The next thing you know, she'll be running for Homecoming queen," Betsy laughed.

"Right!" Laurel exclaimed, sarcastically.

"What's wrong with Melissa running for Homecoming queen?" Izzy demanded. "She's got what it takes."

"Yeah, to lose," Laurel sneered.

"I don't think Melissa would lose," Celeste said, coming to Melissa's defense. "I'll bet she'd even win."

Say something, Melissa chided herself. Don't let them bully you. Don't let Izzy and Celeste fight your battle. Show them you're not afraid. But the words she wanted to say wouldn't come out.

"You're right, Celeste," Izzy agreed. "Melissa would win and I'm going to prove it. This afternoon at assembly I'm going to nominate her for Homecoming queen."

Melissa grabbed Izzy's arm in panic. "Izzy, I don't want to run for Homecoming queen."

Izzy ignored the tight grip Melissa had on her arm. "Yes, you do."

Betsy gave Melissa a nasty smile. "I hope you can handle the competition because I'm nominating Laurel for Homecoming queen."

"And I'm nominating Betsy," Laurel threw in, as the twosome stomped out of the cafeteria. "Westdale needs a queen they can look up to."

"Those two make me so mad!" Izzy fumed. "They think they're so much better than everyone else. I'm sick of the way they rule Westdale."

"You're not going to back out, are you, Melissa?" Celeste asked. "You *are* going to run for Homecoming queen, aren't you?"

Melissa didn't know what to say. On one hand, she was thrilled that she was going to be nominated for Homecoming queen. On the other, she knew if she was nominated, she was going to have to work hard to win votes. No more being shy. And running against Laurel and Betsy wouldn't be easy. They would do whatever it took to win.

But Melissa loved challenges, and she wasn't going to back away from this one. What better way was there for her to get to know people than by running for Homecoming queen?

"Of course I'm going to run for Homecoming queen," Melissa said fiercely. "And I'm going to win!"

"That's the spirit!" Izzy cheered.

"Just think, you may be Westdale High's first Homecoming queen since Brenda Sheldon," Celeste said.

Brenda Sheldon. At the mention of her name, Melissa's blood turned cold. She'd forgotten all about Westdale High's last Homecoming queen. Brenda had been pretty and popular. She'd even had a handsome boyfriend.

But then she'd put on her crown.

And died.

Chapter 3

"Are you sure we're allowed to do this?" Melissa asked as Izzy unlocked the trunk of her father's car. "I thought no one was allowed in school on the weekends."

"You want to win, don't you?" Izzy asked, handing a stack of posters to Melissa and a stack to Celeste. After tucking a stack of posters under her own arm, Izzy slammed the trunk closed and headed for the back entrance of Westdale High. "Your posters will be the first ones up. You'll be the talk of the school."

"But we're not supposed to start putting up posters until Monday morning," Melissa reminded, hurrying after Izzy.

"You don't think Laurel and Betsy are following the rules, do you?" Izzy looked over her shoulder at Melissa with a "get real" expression on her face. "They've probably plastered their posters over every inch of wall space they could find. If they have I'll have to make some of their posters *disappear* so we can put ours up."

"Izzy . . ." Melissa warned.

Izzy sighed. "Like some of your posters aren't going to disappear, Mel? Or they're not going to *accidentally* hang one of their posters over yours?"

"Are you positive we won't get in trouble doing this, Izzy?" Celeste asked. "I don't want anything ending up on my permanent record. Something like that could jeopardize my chances of winning a scholarship."

"That's the fifth time you've asked that question, Celeste," Izzy snapped. "You're driving me nuts! Stop being such a basketcase and chill out. The worst thing that could happen is Principal Phelps makes us take down Melissa's posters."

"That's it? You're sure?" Celeste asked.

Izzy shrugged. "Or he could suspend us."

Celeste's face instantly turned white.

"I was only kidding!" Izzy exclaimed. "We're not going to get suspended."

"But you don't know that for sure," Celeste said, chewing nervously on her lower lip.

"Why don't you stay out here in the car?" Melissa suggested, reaching for the posters under Celeste's arm. "I don't want you doing anything you're uncomfortable with."

"But I want to help you win," Celeste said.

"You already helped me make my posters," Melissa reminded. "And there's going to be lots more to do in the weeks ahead."

"Are you sure?" Celeste asked.

Melissa nodded her head. "I'd feel terrible if I did anything to cost you a scholarship."

A look of relief washed over Celeste's face. "Thanks, Melissa."

"Come on, Mel," Izzy growled. "We've wasted enough time. Let's get to work."

"We'll see you later, Celeste," Melissa called as Celeste headed back in the direction of Izzy's car.

"You didn't have to be so hard on her," Melissa said, joining Izzy's side.

"Sometimes she can be such a baby," Izzy complained. "We're not going to get suspended. All we're doing is getting a jump on the competition. It's not like we're defacing school property."

"How'd you manage to get us into school on a Sunday?" Melissa asked.

"Mr. Hensley, the janitor, plays poker with my father every Saturday night," Izzy explained. "Last night he mentioned he'd be here today with a work crew painting the locker rooms." Izzy pointed across the student parking lot to a pickup truck filled with ladders, tarps, and cans of paint. "See?"

"So?"

"The doors need to be unlocked so the crew can go in and out," Izzy said, opening a steel-gray door.

Melissa followed Izzy into Westdale High. The hallways were dark and the only light available was streaming in from two small windows above the door. The smell of fresh paint and turpentine was thick in the air. "What if someone asks what we're doing here?"

"Who's going to ask? Mr. Hensley's probably in his office watching a baseball game and the crew he hired doesn't know we're not supposed to be here."

"Where do you want to start?" Melissa asked.

"You take the first and second floors and I'll head down to the cafeteria," Izzy instructed.

Melissa walked down a dark hallway, listening to Izzy's footsteps fade away until soon there was total silence. It was an eerie feeling, not hearing any other sounds, and Melissa suddenly felt as though she had been cut off from the rest of the world.

As she walked down the hallway, Melissa couldn't help turning her head and looking over her shoulder. It was strange being in an empty school by herself, not surrounded by the faces she saw every day.

Everything look so different. Deserted.

And dark.

Ever since she was a little girl, Melissa had been afraid of the dark. She was always fearful of something lurking in the shadows.

Hiding under her bed.

Waiting in the closet.

Getting ready to grab her.

Melissa hurried her steps, trying to walk in the center of the hallway, away from the recessed doorways. There was an exit sign over a stairway at the end of the hall and she focused on that. It was the only glimmer of light. Even though the sun was shining brightly outside, there were no windows lining the hallway she was walking down and it was pitch-black.

Deciding to search for a light switch, Melissa reached along the walls with a hand. And even though she knew it was silly, she kept looking over her shoulder. She didn't know why, but she couldn't shake the feeling that someone was staring at her from the darkness.

A second later she heard a sound behind her.

Melissa whirled around, almost dropping her posters, her heart pounding rapidly in her chest. "Is anyone there?" she called out.

She waited for an answer, but didn't get one. *No one's there*, she told herself. Her imagination was playing tricks on her, that was all.

Melissa hurried her search for the light switch, but a second later she heard the sound again. This time she was able to hear it more clearly. It sounded like a footstep.

Could it be Mr. Hensley? Maybe one of the painters?

"Is anyone there?" Melissa asked again. "If you are, please answer me."

Except for the sound of Melissa's voice, the eerie stillness of the hallway remained unbroken.

Finally Melissa's fingers fumbled over a light switch and she flipped it up.

Bright light replaced the darkness and Melissa's racing heart started to slow down. She began to breathe a little easier as her eyes darted around the lit hallway.

No one was in sight.

It had only been her imagination.

Yet Melissa couldn't shake the feeling that it *hadn't* been her imagination.

Could someone have been following her in the darkness?

But who?

Time flew as Melissa began putting up her posters. She was really excited about them and knew they would be different from everyone else's. Izzy had come up with the idea of using fluorescent paints on black poster board so that there would be an almost glow-in-the-dark effect. Her posters would definitely be eye-catching and make her stand out from the other nominees.

They'd spent all day yesterday at Izzy's house working on them. Celeste had offered the use of her house, but Izzy had a basement and they could spread their supplies out.

In order to raise money for Westdale High, votes would be sold. Each vote would cost a dollar and students could buy as many votes as they liked. During the week, a tally would be kept by the student council and every Monday at lunch the results would be posted on a chart in the front of the cafeteria.

Five girls would be competing for Homecoming queen. Besides Melissa, Laurel, and Betsy, two other girls, Faith Robbins and Tia Diaz, had also been nominated. Melissa didn't know Faith or Tia very well, but both had congratulated her on being nominated and they'd seemed friendly.

Still, Melissa knew the competition was going to be tough, especially since Laurel and Betsy were both determined that one of them was going to win.

Ever since the afternoon in the cafeteria when Laurel and Betsy had pretended to be her friends, Melissa's opinion of them had changed. Except when they were with their friends, they were cruel and mean, especially to the less popular students at Westdale High.

After she finished postering the second floor, Melissa headed down to the first floor. She decided to start with the auditorium and began hanging her posters in the back, working her way to the stage. As she moved closer to the front of the auditorium, she saw the stage wasn't empty.

There was a throne in the center of it.

Curious, Melissa abandoned her posters and hurried up the steps that ran along the side of the stage.

The throne was made of carved dark wood with a high arched back, curving arms, and a plush green satin seat. Draped across the seat was a red velvet robe trimmed with white fur.

On top of the robe were a crown and a scepter.

Melissa fingered the soft velvet of the robe. Was the drama club getting ready to start a new production? Usually they didn't begin casting and rehearsals until November.

Melissa picked up the crown carefully, not wanting to break it. It was made of gold, glittering with shiny red, blue, and green stones. Slowly she placed it on top of her head. It fit perfectly.

Next she slipped the red velvet robe around her shoulders and picked up the scepter. It was long and thin, made of silver with a pointed tip.

There was a full-length mirror from last spring's play in the corner of the stage. Turning to the mirror, Melissa began admiring herself. She looked like a queen. A Homecoming queen.

Melissa closed her eyes, sitting down on the throne, imagining what it would be like to be crowned Westdale High's Homecoming queen.

It would be a magical night, perfect for romance. Seth would be crowned Homecoming king and they would spend the entire night together. Then when the Homecoming dance was over and he took her home, he would take her in his arms and kiss her. Again and again. It would be a wonderful way to end a perfect evening. No one would ever dread Homecoming again, and the memory of Brenda Sheldon would be put to rest forever.

At the thought of Brenda Sheldon, chills traveled down Melissa's spine. Her eyes popped open as she stared at the throne she was sitting on. Was this the same throne Brenda Sheldon had sat on when she was Homecoming queen?

Melissa brought a hand to the crown on her head and looked at the robe she was wearing. Had Brenda worn this crown and robe? She gazed at the scepter in her lap. Had she held this same scepter only hours before she died?

Suddenly the silence of the auditorium was broken by a whizzing sound, jarring Melissa out of her thoughts.

Startled, she looked up.

And saw a sandbag headed straight for her head.

Chapter 4

Melissa jumped off the throne.

A second later the sandbag crashed down on the spot where she'd been sitting.

Smashing the throne to pieces.

Goose bumps broke out along Melissa's arms and she started to shake at the thought of the heavy sandbag crashing down onto her skull.

If she hadn't heard the sandbag falling . . .

If she hadn't jumped off the throne in time . . .

She could have been killed.

Just like the last Homecoming queen.

Suddenly Melissa couldn't stand wearing the crown on her head. She ripped it off and threw it to the floor, followed by the red velvet robe and scepter.

Melissa raced off the stage and up the center aisle of the auditorium, needing to get outside.

She didn't want to be alone anymore and had to find Izzy and Celeste. Too many creepy things had happened this afternoon.

Once outside, Melissa sat down on the front steps and took a deep breath. It was still Indian summer, and the weather was quite warm. Closing her eyes, she raised her face to the sun, enjoying its warmth.

After a few minutes, Melissa began to feel much better and was just getting ready to search for Izzy and Celeste when she heard someone approaching.

"What are you doing here?" Betsy demanded.

Shielding her eyes from the sun with an open hand, Melissa gazed up at Betsy. "Putting up posters."

"We're not supposed to hang any posters until tomorrow," Betsy said, a displeased expression on her face.

"Then what are *you* doing here?" Melissa asked, rising to her feet. "And what are those under your arm?"

"They're posters," a voice from behind Melissa said. "Got a problem with that?"

Melissa jumped at the unexpected sound of Zach's voice. As he walked through the front doors of Westdale High, he gave her a surly look. Melissa had always disliked Zach. It wasn't that he'd done anything to her personally, but he had such a monster ego! With his jet-black hair and ice-blue eyes, he was strikingly handsome — and knew it. His body was well-toned from all the hours he spent working out. He always seemed to be posing, expecting girls to fall at his feet. Not only was he captain of the varsity football and baseball teams, but he also ran track and was on the swim team.

What really bothered Melissa about Zach was the way he treated Betsy. Like he owned her. He never let her out of his sight and went ballistic if another guy even looked at her. Melissa knew Betsy thrived on the attention Zach gave her, but in her opinion their relationship was a little too twisted. She wouldn't want any guy to be obsessed with her the way Zach was obsessed with Betsy. It reminded her too much of *Fatal Attraction*.

"I don't know why you're even bothering to run for Homecoming queen," Zach said, wrapping an arm around Betsy's shoulder and giving her a kiss. "You're looking at Westdale High's next Homecoming queen. Betsy's going to win. I'm going to make sure of it, so you might as well drop out of the running."

There was no mistaking the confidence in Zach's voice. The smugness. "I might have something to say about that," Melissa said. She tried to speak forcefully, so it wouldn't seem like she was being intimidated. "And the other nominees, too."

"I know how to take care of competition," Zach said, his blue eyes darkening as he cracked his knuckles.

Just then Laurel stuck her head out the front doors. "What's keeping you, Zach? Did you track down Betsy?" Laurel's gaze fell upon Melissa and a crafty smile crossed her lips. "Oh, hi, Melissa. I'm surprised to see you here on a Sunday."

Melissa saw the stack of posters Laurel had under her arm. There was no mistaking the black background or neon colors. "Those are mine," Melissa accused, hurrying up the steps and snatching her posters away from Laurel. "If I find out you've taken down any of my posters or messed with them, I'm going straight to the student council," she warned.

"I didn't take down any of your posters," Laurel sneered. "I found these on the floor in the auditorium."

"Laurel doesn't need to take down your posters," Betsy added. "Don't you know it's going to take more than posters to win?"

Melissa knew Laurel and Betsy were just trying to psyche her out, but she wasn't going to let their words get to her. "We'll see who's wasting their time when the first votes are taken tomorrow."

Leaving Laurel, Betsy, and Zach behind on the steps, Melissa headed for the student parking lot. There she found Izzy leaning against the side of her car, munching on a candy bar, while Celeste was flipping through an SAT prep book, checking the answers to a test she'd taken.

"You still didn't finish?" Izzy asked, breaking off a string of caramel between her mouth and the candy bar in her hand.

"I almost had an accident," Melissa explained.

Celeste looked up from her test book. "Accident? What kind of accident?"

Without wasting any time, Melissa told Izzy and Celeste what had happened in the auditorium.

"You don't think it could have anything to do with Brenda Sheldon, do you?" Celeste asked, her fingers curling tightly around the edges of her test book.

"What do you mean?" Melissa asked.

"Maybe it was her ghost," Celeste said. "If you were wearing her crown and robe and sitting on her throne, maybe she got angry. Maybe she wanted to punish you."

Izzy popped the rest of her candy bar into her mouth and laughed. "Come on, Celeste. Get real! How superstitious are you? It was an accident, that's all. Whoever was manning the curtains last didn't tie back the cord holding the sandbag tight enough."

Celeste shrugged. "Laugh if you want, Izzy, but maybe Brenda Sheldon's ghost is upset that Westdale High's going to have a Homecoming queen again."

"Ghosts don't exist," Izzy said firmly, opening the driver's door and sliding behind the steering wheel. "I've got to head home and study for a quiz. Is it okay if we put up the rest of your posters tomorrow, Mel?"

"Sure," Melissa answered, sliding into the passenger seat and fastening her seat belt.

During the drive Melissa was quiet. She kept thinking about the fallen sandbag. Had it been deliberate? She really didn't believe Celeste's theory, but she had come up with a theory of her own, one that she wasn't ready to share yet.

Both Zach and Laurel had been inside Westdale High the same time as she had. Had one of them been trying to scare her and perhaps get her out of the running? After all, Zach had said he knew how to take care of the competition.

Melissa didn't know for sure, but it wouldn't hurt to be on her guard until the race for Homecoming queen was over.

But she was overreacting, wasn't she? It had been an accident.

Hadn't it?

Chapter 5

Melissa's posters were a huge hit. And she owed it all to Izzy.

Somehow, before first period, Izzy managed to turn off all the lights in the school. As students made their way to classes, the neon colors of Melissa's posters popped out and danced in the dark, while the posters of the other Homecoming queen nominees couldn't even be seen.

The rest of the morning, wherever Melissa went, students kept congratulating her on her posters.

Now it was lunchtime and Melissa was waiting for the results of the first round of voting.

"I'm so nervous," Melissa confessed to Celeste, pushing away her lunch tray. She hadn't been able to eat a thing. "What if no one votes for me?"

"Izzy and I voted for you. Twice. That's four votes. And then there's your vote. Five."

Melissa clasped a hand over her mouth. "I forgot to vote for myself!"

Celeste laughed. "That's no way to win!"

"Win what?" Izzy asked, sitting down next to Celeste.

"Melissa forgot to vote for herself," Celeste said.

Izzy flashed a mysterious smile. "I don't think one vote is going to make much of a difference."

"What have you heard?" Melissa asked, trying not to sound too eager.

"Principal Phelps is trying to find out who turned off the electricity this morning," Izzy said, spooning into a container of strawberry yogurt.

"How *did* you do that?" Melissa asked.

Izzy waved a hand. "I threw the main switch in the boiler room. Nothing to it."

"That was a big risk," Celeste said. "If he finds out you were the one, you could be —"

"I know, I know," Izzy said, cutting her off. "I could be suspended. But it paid off. Everyone was talking about Melissa's posters."

"Hear anything else?" Melissa asked.

"The student council is really excited," Izzy said. "They're making lots of money selling votes."

Celeste jabbed Izzy in the side. "That's not what Melissa wants to know and you know it!"

"Come on, Izzy," Melissa begged. "Don't keep me in suspense."

Izzy took a bite of her apple. "They're saying it looks like you're in the lead."

Celeste clapped her hands. "Yay!"

"No," Melissa gasped, unable to believe it. "Really?"

Izzy nodded her head. "Really, but you've got to keep that lead, Melissa. The posters were a start, but I've come up with another idea."

"What is it?"

"Fortune cookies! We'll make up fortunes that say VOTE FOR MELISSA and bake them into cookies. Then we'll hand them out."

"Look!" Celeste exclaimed. "Kim's headed for the mike."

Izzy crossed her fingers. "This is it, Mel!"

Kimberly Hanson, Westdale High's student council president, walked up to the microphone at the front of the cafeteria. Behind her was a blackboard with five columns, and above each column was the name of a different girl competing for Homecoming queen.

Silence fell over the cafeteria as Kim leaned over the mike, tossing her long, curly black hair over one shoulder. "First, I want to thank everyone for being so generous," she began. "We've raised a hundred dollars so far." Claps and whoops broke out through the cafeteria. "And I want to remind everyone that there's plenty of time to vote, and you can vote as often as you like. Each vote only costs a dollar."

Melissa gazed across the cafeteria at a table where Laurel and Betsy were sitting. Both looked pretty tense. Could Izzy be right? Was she in the lead? Melissa turned her eyes back to Kim. She'd know in just a few seconds.

Kimberly turned to the blackboard behind her and picked up a piece of chalk, moving from column to column. Under each nominee's name, she wrote a number. When she finished and stepped away, there was a mad rush to the front of the cafeteria.

"You go look, Izzy," Melissa said. "I can't."

Izzy disappeared while Celeste clutched Melissa's hand reassuringly. "Are you doing anything this afternoon?"

Melissa shook her head. "Nothing."

"Want to come over to my house? I'm working on an essay for a college application and I want to see what you think of it. We could listen to CDs, too."

"Sure," Melissa said. "We'll meet after last period."

"Melissa, you're in the lead!" Izzy cried, rushing back to the table.

Melissa's mouth dropped open. "I am?"

Izzy grinned. "You are!"

"How does everyone else stack up?"

"Faith is in second place and Tia is in third."

"That means . . ." Celeste began, a smile spreading across her face.

Izzy laughed. "That's right. The Gruesome Twosome are in fourth and fifth."

Melissa couldn't believe it. She was in the lead, ahead of Laurel and Betsy! Melissa scanned the crowded cafeteria, trying to catch a glimpse of them and see what their reaction was, but they were nowhere in sight.

Five minutes later, on the way to her locker to get books for her afternoon classes, Melissa ran into Laurel and Betsy. Neither one was smiling.

"What'd you do, Melissa? Break open your piggy bank and use your snack money to buy votes?" Laurel asked.

"Sour grapes, Laurel?" Izzy asked while Melissa and Celeste remained silent.

"I wasn't talking to you, Isabel," Laurel said, knowing Izzy hated being called by her full name.

"Don't you ever look at yourself in a mirror in the morning?" Betsy asked. "You're so clueless when it comes to clothes. You're nothing but a Fashion Don't."

"What's wrong with what I have on?" Izzy demanded. Today she was wearing a red satin bowling shirt, black leggings, and saddle shoes.

"You look like you just came from the fifties," Betsy said.

Laurel tugged on Betsy's arm. "We're wasting time with these losers. Let's get to class."

Melissa didn't know where she found the courage to talk back to Laurel, but she did. "You're calling *me* a loser, Laurel? I'm not the one in last place."

Laurel gave Melissa a dark look. "What happened today was a fluke. You probably got the sympathy vote this week, but if I were you, I wouldn't get too used to being in the lead because *I'm* going to be Westdale High's next Homecoming queen." Laurel jabbed a finger at Melissa's chest. "No matter what it takes."

"Your majesty," Seth said, bowing before Melissa as she walked into anatomy class.

Melissa giggled. "You may rise."

"Congrats on your lead," he said as they headed to their seats.

"Congratulations to you, too." Only four guys had been nominated for Homecoming king, and Seth was among them. So far, he was in the lead. "Who do you think your queen will be?"

"You, of course,"

"Thanks, but it's too early to tell if I'm really going to win."

"You got twenty votes from me."

Melissa almost fell off the stool she was sliding onto. "Twenty votes?"

Seth hopped onto the stool next to Melissa and opened his spiral-bound notebook. "Twenty votes."

Don't jump to conclusions, Melissa told herself. He didn't spend twenty dollars on *me*. He bought the tickets because it's for a good cause and he felt sorry for me. He didn't want me embarrassing myself in front of the whole school. That's all.

Laurel's words echoed in Melissa's mind: *You probably got the sympathy vote*. Was that true? Had people voted for her because they felt sorry for her? It didn't seem that way. The last couple of days, wherever she went, students came up to her. They went out of their way to say hi and chat for a few minutes, congratulating her on her nomination. The more it happened, the easier she found it. She'd even started joining some after-school clubs and committees.

"You didn't have to do that," Melissa said to Seth. "One vote would have been enough."

"But I wanted to. You deserve to win."

Melissa pretended to look for a pen in her shoulder bag. She didn't know what to say. Why was he being so nice to her? "Thanks."

"Your posters are really cool."

"My friend Izzy came up with the concept."

"Is she the one always wearing those funky clothes?"

"Uh-huh."

"She seems like one of a kind."

"That's Izzy. So, Seth, how come you never used to talk to me?" Melissa blurted out, not knowing where the words came from, only that they were flowing out of her mouth uncontrollably. "Was it because of the way I used to look?"

For a second, Seth looked stunned by her words. But then he found his voice, and it was angry. "How can you say that?"

"It's true, isn't it? Last semester you didn't even know I was alive."

"That's not true and I can prove it," Seth

said. "I actually know a lot about you."

"Like what?" Melissa challenged.

Seth began counting off on his fingers. "You like reading Stephen King, your favorite magazine is *Glamour*. Your favorite band is Smashing Pumpkins and your favorite actor is Brad Pitt. You like blueberry yogurt, chocolate-chip cookies, and cookie-dough ice cream, but you hate bananas, tapioca pudding, and brussels sprouts."

Melissa was amazed. "How do you know all that about me?"

Seth crossed his arms over his chest. "Easy. I'm very observant. You might not have noticed me last semester, but I noticed you."

I noticed you all the time, Melissa wanted to say. Instead she asked, "So why didn't you ever talk to me?"

Seth sighed. "When I was dating Laurel, it was tough. She would freak out if she saw me talking with other girls, and she made things pretty tough for them."

"Is that why you broke up with her?"

"One of the reasons. She always liked being in control, making our plans, deciding who our friends would be. None of that stuff matters to me. I guess as I got to know her better, I didn't like her very much. I don't like anyone telling me who I can be friends with. By the end of the summer I'd had enough and broke up with her."

"But she wants you back," Melissa pointed out.

"That's because *I* ended things with her," Seth explained. "Laurel's never been dumped before; she's always been the dumper."

"She says the two of you are getting back together."

Seth shook his head adamantly. "It's not going to happen."

"Why not?"

"I think it's time for a new girlfriend." Seth raised an eyebrow at Melissa and gave her a mischievous smile as he started doodling on a page in his notebook. "Know anyone who's interested?"

Me, me, me! Melissa wanted to shout. But she was saved from answering by the arrival of Ms. Kazmier, who instructed the class to put away all their books and take out a sheet of paper for a surprise quiz.

Forty-five minutes later, as the dismissal bell rang, there was a rumble of thunder from outside. Looking out a window, Melissa saw thick storm clouds gathering in the sky.

"Sounds like it's getting ready to pour,"

Seth said, as he and Melissa walked out of Ms. Kazmier's class and into a hallway filled with the sound of clanging lockers. "How 'bout I give you a ride home?"

"Only if it's not out of your way," Melissa said, trying not to sound too excited.

"I'll meet you out front in ten minutes?"

"Ten minutes," Melissa said.

Once Seth was out of sight, Melissa raced to her locker. She couldn't wait to tell Izzy and Celeste that she was getting a ride home with Seth.

Celeste! How could she have forgotten? She'd promised to go over to her house this afternoon and help her work on an essay.

Melissa scanned the crowded hallways as students dashed to their lockers, but she didn't see Celeste anywhere.

After switching her books, Melissa waited in front of Celeste's locker. Checking the time on her watch, Melissa saw she was ten minutes late. She couldn't leave Seth waiting any longer. Scribbling a note, Melissa slipped it through one of the vents in Celeste's locker. Hopefully she'd see it.

"Sorry I'm late," Melissa apologized when she reached Seth's car.

"No problem," he said, opening the passenger door. "Hop in."

Melissa slid into the buttery soft interior of Seth's red Honda just as the first big drops of rain began to fall.

"How do you think you did on Kazmier's quiz?" Seth asked as he pulled out into the street and turned on the windshield wipers.

"So-so," Melissa answered, fastening her seat belt. "I think I missed a few questions."

"Want the radio on?" Seth asked.

"No thanks. Unless you do."

Seth stopped at a red light. "I'd rather talk. What was it like working as a camp counselor?"

"Hard, but fun," Melissa said. "I want to do it again next year."

"Your summer sounds better than mine," Seth said as the light turned green and he continued driving.

"What'd you do?"

"Vegged out at the beach during the day and vegged out with the TV after dinner," Seth said, pulling up his car in front of the town library and turning off the engine. "We'd better park here until it lets up." The rain was coming down harder, in thick sheets, and visibility was close to zero. "You know, you never answered my question in Kazmier's class."

Melissa stole a peek at Seth out of the corner of her eye. "What question was that?"

A smile curled around the edges of his lips. "You know which one."

Melissa pretended to think for a second. "About a new girlfriend? We haven't even gone out on a date."

"Good point," Seth agreed. "Want to go to the county fair next Saturday?"

Did she?! Melissa's stomach did flip-flops at the thought.

Seth moved closer to Melissa. She wondered what it would be like to burrow close to him and have him wrap his arms around her.

"Is it a date?" Seth asked, leaning over Melissa and pressing his lips lightly against hers.

"It's a date," Melissa whispered.

Melissa got drenched racing to her front porch when Seth dropped her off, but she didn't care. They had a date!

Once inside, Melissa slipped out of her wet clothes and into dry ones. Toweling her hair, she headed down to the kitchen and popped two pieces of bread into the toaster.

While waiting for the bread to toast, Melissa flipped through the day's mail. The latest issue of *Sassy* had arrived, as well as a letter from Mike. The letter wasn't very long — just a short and chatty note — but it was nice hearing from him.

Melissa's toast popped up and she smeared both slices with peanut butter and jelly. Then she filled a glass with milk and carried it all into the living room.

Her two cats, Salt and Pepper, joined her on the couch as she was aiming the remote control at the TV. "Hey, guys."

With Salt and Pepper nestled on each side of her while she munched on her snack, Melissa flipped through the channels before settling on a soap opera. She was deeply engrossed in watching two sisters fight over the same guy when the phone rang.

"Hello," Melissa said, trying to talk clearly around the peanut butter in her mouth.

"Melissa, where were you?" Celeste wailed. "I waited over an hour at school. I thought you were going to come over to my house."

"I'm really sorry, Celeste. I tried to find you after last period but it was a mob scene."

"I got stuck in the guidance office talking to Miss Persky. She kept me for twenty minutes," Celeste complained. "When I got out I thought I'd find you waiting at my locker. What happened?"

Melissa couldn't wait to share her news. "Seth Powell gave me a ride home," she gushed.

"That's why you couldn't come over to my house?" Celeste asked incredulously.

"I left a note in your locker. I guess you didn't see it."

"No, I didn't."

"Celeste, don't be mad," Melissa begged, although she couldn't blame her. She *had* promised to go over to her house. "You know how much I like Seth. I forgot that I'd promised to help you this afternoon and when I did remember I thought if I didn't accept his offer for a ride, he'd never ask again. Don't you understand?"

"I guess so," Celeste grudgingly admitted. "How'd it go?"

Melissa flopped down on the couch, causing Salt and Pepper to jump to the floor. "Great! We're going to the county fair next Saturday."

"I'm really happy for you," Celeste said, although to Melissa's ear she didn't sound very happy.

"Celeste, I'm really sorry about this afternoon, but wait till you hear what else happened."

"What?"

"He kissed me!"

Celeste shrieked on the other end of the line. "Way to go! Why don't you come over tonight and you can tell me all about it."

"I can't," Melissa said. "I've got a paper for English class that I have to work on. Tomorrow?"

"Sounds good. I'll talk to you later."

" 'Bye," Melissa said, and hung up.

That night after dinner, Melissa wrote a letter back to Mike, telling him all about her nomination for Homecoming queen and her upcoming date with Seth. When the letter was finished, she dropped it off in the corner mailbox and then headed over to the library to work on her English paper.

It had stopped raining earlier in the evening, and the streets and sidewalks were slick and wet. Crystal-clear droplets hung from orange, red, yellow, and gold leaves on the trees. Dripping to the ground, they looked like diamonds glittering in the silver moonlight.

Outside the library Melissa stared at the spot where she and Seth had parked that afternoon. She ran her fingers over her lips, remembering the way his kiss had felt. She shivered with pleasure, wondering what it would be like the next time he kissed her (if there *was* a next time!).

Inside the library Melissa found a table in a corner, inhaling the musty smell of the books around her. If there was one smell she loved above all else, it was the smell of books.

She had just started flipping through her highlighted copy of *Othello*, jotting down notes, when she looked up and saw Faith Robbins and Tia Diaz headed her way.

Faith was petite, with a creamy complexion sprinkled with freckles and a cap of short brown hair. Tia was dark-skinned, with shoulder-length hair that was jet black, and usually worn in a French braid.

"Hi, we thought it was you," Tia said with a smile, tossing her backpack on the table. "Mind if we join you?"

"Congrats on being in the lead," Faith said, sliding into the seat across from Melissa.

"Thanks."

"What are you working on?" Tia asked.

"I have to do a paper on Shakespeare's villains. Compare and contrast."

"So do I!" Faith exclaimed. "Do you have Griswald for English?"

"Second period."

"I've got him for fourth. He's so-o-o boring."

"Did you see Laurel's face at lunch when the votes were posted?" Tia whispered, noticing Mrs. Babcock, the librarian, glaring in their direction. "I've never seen her so mad."

"I can't stand her!" Faith said.

"How come?" Melissa asked.

"She and Betsy kept me off the cheerleading squad last year. They said my moves weren't fresh enough, but that wasn't the real reason I didn't make the squad." Faith continued. "I had to work on a group project with Seth Powell in American history and Laurel thought I was trying to steal him from her."

"Were you?" Melissa asked.

Faith giggled. "Of course!"

"But that was no reason to blackball you from the squad," Tia said.

"Are you and Seth an item?" Faith asked. "I saw you get in his car after school."

Melissa answered cautiously, knowing Faith loved to gossip. "We're just friends."

"Have you heard the news about Brenda Sheldon?" Faith whispered. "They say she's going to return the night of the Homecoming dance, ready to reclaim her crown. And if she can't get it off the Homecoming queen's head, she's going to tear the head off, too!"

"Then let's hope Laurel is crowned queen," Tia laughed.

"Have you shopped for a dress for the dance yet?" Faith asked.

For the next hour Melissa, Faith, and Tia talked about boys, clothes, movies, school, and music. Melissa found herself liking them both and was disappointed when Faith had to leave.

"Do you want a ride home, Tia?" Faith asked, packing her books. "I've got my car."

"Okay," Tia said, jumping to her feet.

"How about you, Melissa?"

"Thanks, but I've got to get a chunk of this paper done."

"I'm having a party in two weeks," Faith added. "Friday night. I hope you can come."

Another invitation — her second in the same day! This had never happened to her last semester. Was she on her way to becoming popular?

Melissa didn't have any other plans that night. Izzy had mentioned maybe having a video marathon at her house, but nothing had been definite. That meant she could accept Faith's invitation, didn't it?

"Can you make it, Melissa?" Faith asked.

"I'd love to!" Melissa rushed to answer.

"Great!" Faith said. "See you in school tomorrow."

Melissa waved good night to Faith and Tia as they headed out the door and focused her attention back on her paper until the library closed an hour later.

Standing on the deserted steps of the library, Melissa found herself wishing she'd accepted Faith's offer of a ride. It had started raining again, lightly this time, and the streets were dark. A strong wind was blowing, and Melissa shivered as it seeped under her thin cotton sweater. She began walking as fast as she could. All she could think about was getting home and snuggling up in bed with Salt and Pepper, sipping a piping hot cup of cocoa.

The houses she passed were all dark and Melissa found herself wanting it to be Christmas. If the houses were decorated with bright, twinkling lights, it wouldn't seem so spooky out.

Because the weather was awful, no one was on the streets. Melissa was nervous being out by herself and couldn't help thinking someone was behind her.

She crossed onto a block that ran along a patch of woods. There were no streetlights, and thick gloomy shadows stretched across the street, throwing strange shapes in Melissa's path, but she kept her eyes glued in front of her, hurrying her pace, not wanting to look toward the trees.

She'd reached the end of the block and was crossing the street when she heard the sound of snapping branches.

Melissa instantly stood still, listening intently, trying to figure out where the sound was coming from. But except for the wind, all was silent.

She started walking again, but then she heard the snapping sound again.

And again.

It was coming from across the street.

Stopping in her tracks, Melissa turned around slowly and blinked disbelieving eyes.

Standing in the woods was a figure wearing a tattered white dress splattered with blood.

The figure pointed a finger at Melissa. A reed-thin voice traveled through the night, cutting through Melissa and chilling her to the bone.

"Wear the crown and you will die . . . die *just like me.*"

Chapter 6

Melissa couldn't believe her eyes.

It was the ghost of Brenda Sheldon.

Paralyzed by fear, Melissa stood motionless in the middle of the street. Then, from behind, she heard the blare of a car's horn. Tearing her eyes away from the figure in the woods, Melissa whirled around and saw a pair of headlights headed straight for her.

Move, her mind screamed.

With a burst of adrenaline, Melissa jumped back onto the sidewalk just as the car whizzed by.

Heart pounding frantically in her chest, Melissa turned her gaze back to the woods.

What she saw took her breath away.

No one was there.

The ghost was gone.

Had she imagined it?

No, she couldn't have. She'd heard the

voice, the voice of Brenda Sheldon.

She was almost tempted to cross the street and look in the woods, but couldn't. She was too scared. What if something was hiding in the shadows, waiting to grab her?

Waiting to make sure she wasn't crowned Homecoming queen.

Taking one final look at the dark woods, Melissa turned her back and ran all the way home.

Izzy, wearing bell-bottom jeans, a tie-dyed T-shirt, and platform shoes, was waiting for Melissa at her locker the following morning.

"In a seventies mood today?" Melissa asked, opening her locker.

"We can talk about my fabulous frocks later," Izzy said. "What's this I hear about you and Seth locking lips yesterday afternoon?"

"It was only a kiss," Melissa said, emptying her backpack and searching for the books she needed for her morning classes.

"*Only* a kiss? I heard he asked you out."

"Who told you all that? Celeste?"

"I didn't tell anyone except Izzy," Celeste said, coming up from behind Melissa and crossing her heart. "I swear."

Izzy leaned against the locker next to Melissa's. "You look awful."

"I didn't get much sleep last night," Melissa confessed.

"How come?" Celeste asked.

Melissa looked around the hallway, not wanting to be overheard. "If I tell you guys something, will you keep it a secret?" she asked in a low voice.

"You can trust me," Izzy said.

"Me, too," Celeste said.

Melissa took a deep breath. "Last night, on my way home from the library, I saw Brenda Sheldon's ghost."

With those words, Melissa began her story. By the time she had finished, Celeste was wide-eyed and pale while Izzy had an incredulous look on her face.

"You're not serious, are you, Melissa?" Izzy asked.

"I know what I saw, Izzy."

"There's no such thing as ghosts."

"Then what did I see last night?" Melissa demanded.

"Someone was playing a joke on you."

"Who would do such a thing?" Celeste asked.

"Two guesses," Izzy said, pointing a finger at Laurel and Betsy as they sauntered down the hallway, surrounded by their usual clique.

"Why?" Melissa asked.

"To get back at you," Celeste said. "Word is spreading that Seth gave you a ride home."

Melissa groaned. "It was only a ride."

"Imagine if she knew about the kiss," Izzy added. "If I were you, I wouldn't mention this to anyone. It could cost you votes. Pretend it never happened. Laurel is probably expecting you to freak out. When you don't, it'll drive her crazy."

"I guess you're right," Melissa said, feeling a little bit better. "It does make sense."

"Don't look now," Izzy whispered, "but lover boy is headed our way. We'll see you later." Izzy and Celeste hurried down the hall.

"Hi, Melissa. On your way to homeroom?"

Melissa swung her backpack over one shoulder and slammed her locker shut. "I am now."

"Doing anything Friday afternoon?" Seth asked as they started walking together.

"I don't have any plans," Melissa said. "Why? Did you have something in mind?"

"Do you like Rollerblading?"

"I love it."

"Want to go to Westdale Park?"

"That'd be fun."

"Cool," Seth said as they walked into homeroom. "We'll talk later and set up the details."

Seth headed for his desk in the fifth row

while Melissa slid into her seat in the first row. She had hardly sat down before Izzy and Celeste were clustered around her.

"Quick, there's still a few minutes before the final bell rings," Izzy said. "What did he want?"

"Seth asked me to go Rollerblading with him Friday afternoon."

"Did you turn him down?" Izzy asked.

"Of course not!" Melissa exclaimed. "Why would I turn him down?"

"We're supposed to go shopping at the mall Friday afternoon. To look for dresses for the Homecoming dance, remember?"

Melissa felt her cheeks turn red. "I forgot."

"You seem to be doing a lot of that lately," Izzy complained. "Celeste told me the way you blew her off yesterday afternoon. Are you becoming a member of the snob squad or what?"

"I didn't blow her off and I'm not a snob," Melissa said hotly. "When it comes to Seth I forget things. I'm sorry. I'll cancel my date with him."

"Why don't we go shopping this afternoon?" Celeste suggested.

"If we went shopping this afternoon, you could still keep your date with Seth on Friday," Izzy said. "I wouldn't want you to break it."

"Are you sure?" Melissa asked.

Izzy nodded her head. "I didn't mean to lose my temper. Friends?"

Melissa smiled. "Best."

After school Melissa, Izzy, and Celeste headed straight for the mall.

"What kind of dress do you want to get, Melissa?" Celeste asked as they took the escalator to the second floor.

"Something that Seth will never forget!"

"You really like him, don't you?"

"At least his taste in girlfriends has improved," Izzy commented.

"I'm not his girlfriend," Melissa said.

"Yet," Izzy said, smiling. "Hey, check out that dress." Izzy pointed to a low-cut, strapless red dress in the window of a boutique they were passing. "Seth would never forget you in a dress like that."

"Don't you think it's a little too sexy?" Celeste commented.

"I agree," Melissa said. Although the dress *was* a knockout, it was very revealing, unlike anything she'd ever worn before. "Besides, my dad would never let me out of the house in it."

A naughty look filled Izzy's blue eyes. "We could always buy it and keep it at my house."

Melissa stared at the dress thoughtfully. "My parents are going away on the weekend of the Homecoming dance. There wouldn't be a chance of me getting caught in it."

"Come on, let's go in and you can try it on," Izzy urged, steering Melissa in the direction of the boutique's entrance.

Once inside the boutique, Melissa and Celeste began looking through the racks while Izzy went to find a sales clerk.

"How about this?" Celeste asked, showing Melissa an ivory-colored dress.

The sight of the dress made Melissa's skin crawl. It reminded her too much of the dress the figure in the woods had been wearing the night before. "I want something in a darker color," Melissa said, not wanting to tell Celeste the real reason why she didn't like the dress.

By the time Izzy returned with a sales clerk, Melissa had found a jade-green dress with spaghetti straps that wasn't as revealing as the red dress in the window.

"I've changed my mind, Izzy," she said, holding up the dress she'd picked out. "I'm going to try this one on."

Izzy yawned. "B-o-r-ing."

"It's not so bad," Celeste said. "With the right shoes — "

Izzy cut Celeste off. "I thought you wanted to impress Seth."

"I do," Melissa said.

"Then at least try on the red dress," Izzy begged. "Please?"

Melissa finally gave in and headed to the dressing room with the red dress and the jade-green dress she liked. On her way into the dressing room she bumped into Laurel, who was on her way out with Betsy.

"Sorry," Melissa said, trying to make her way around them.

"Shopping for a Homecoming dress, Melissa?" Laurel asked, peeking at the two dresses Melissa was holding. "I wouldn't bother." She pointed to the sparkly silver dress draped over her arm. "I'm buying the best dress in the shop."

"It's very pretty," Melissa said.

"I hope you don't spend a lot of money on a dress because you think you're going to be Homecoming queen," Betsy said. "You got lucky this week."

"We'll see what happens next week, won't we?" Melissa said.

Izzy stuck her head between the blue velvet curtains of the dressing room. "Melissa, what's keeping you? Are you going to keep Seth waiting this long the night of the dance?"

Laurel looked at Melissa with shock. "*You're* going to the Homecoming dance with Seth?"

"No," Melissa said, wishing Izzy hadn't opened her big mouth. Seth hadn't even asked her to the Homecoming dance.

"Then why do you think he'd even ask you?"

"Because they're going Rollerblading on Friday afternoon and to the county fair next Saturday," Izzy said smugly.

Izzy's words only made Laurel angrier. "I told you Seth was off-limits."

"It doesn't matter what you told me," Melissa said softly. "He's not your boyfriend anymore, Laurel."

Laurel pushed her way past Melissa but turned around at the dressing room door. "We'll see who gets Seth and we'll see who becomes Homecoming queen. There are still two weeks left to the competition, Melissa. Anything can happen in that time. *Anything*."

Chapter 7

"I still say you should have bought the red dress," Izzy insisted.

"Don't listen to her, Melissa," Celeste said as they left the boutique. "The dress you bought is gorgeous. Green is your color. Seth is going to flip."

"Thanks, Celeste." Melissa didn't say anything to Izzy. She hadn't said a word to her since Laurel and Betsy left the dressing room. Although Izzy had offered comments while she'd tried on both dresses, Melissa had ignored her while admiring herself in a three-sectioned mirror. She was still too angry over the way Izzy had told Laurel about her dates with Seth.

"Mel, don't be mad," Izzy pleaded.

Melissa finally broke her silence. "Why shouldn't I be? You couldn't wait to blab to Laurel about Seth and me."

"She would have found out eventually."

"Eventually didn't have to be today. You've made her even angrier. Who knows what she'll pull next to get back at me? Why do you hate her so much?"

"I can answer that," Celeste piped up. "When Izzy was a sophomore she used to have a crush on a senior named David Wilson. Laurel found out about it and started sending notes to Izzy, making her think they were from David. When Izzy finally worked up the courage to tell David how she felt about him, he laughed at her and told all his friends."

"The entire school laughed at me," Izzy said bitterly, her cheeks turning red with anger. "It was so humiliating! You can't just play with other people's emotions. It's not right. But Laurel didn't care. She wanted to make me look like a fool."

Melissa's heart ached for Izzy and the pain she'd gone through. "I'm sorry."

A determined look washed over Izzy's face. "I've never forgotten what Laurel did to me. I promised myself that one day I'd get even with her. And I will. Somehow, I will."

"Can't we forget about Laurel and Betsy and Homecoming?" Celeste asked. "Let's have some fun and shop."

"Sounds good to me," Melissa agreed,

hooking an arm through Izzy's to let her know she wasn't mad at her anymore. "But you know what I need before we get started? A sugar fix!"

They stopped into a candy shop called The Sweet Tooth. The sweet aroma of chocolate wafting in the air made Melissa's mouth water.

"Hey, Melissa, I just had a brainstorm," Izzy said, showing her a handful of silver-wrapped chocolate kisses. "Why don't we buy some of these? We can replace the white slip that's inside with one that says 'A Kiss from Your Queen.'"

"That's a great idea," Celeste agreed, nibbling on a strand of red licorice. "And you know those candy hearts that have sayings on them? Why don't we buy some? We could call Melissa the Queen of Hearts, and she could hand them out."

"Yeah," Izzy agreed. "We'll have a vote for Melissa in almost every stomach at Westdale High!" As the three girls approached the cash register, they ran into Faith and Tia.

"Hi, Melissa," Faith said, checking out the filled basket under her arm. "Getting some munchies?"

"Yeah. Do you know my friends Izzy and Celeste?" Melissa asked.

"Nice to meet you. Listen, Melissa," Faith said. "I forgot to tell you what time my party starts. Eight o'clock. I'll give you directions on how to get to my house the day before the party."

Faith and Tia chatted with Melissa a little bit longer and then waved good-bye. The second they were out of the store, Izzy pounced. "Party? What party?"

Melissa put the basket of candy on the counter for the cashier to bag. "Faith is having a party and invited me."

"Since when are you friends with them?" There was a hostile tone in Izzy's voice.

Melissa paid for the candy and accepted a shopping bag from the cashier. "Why can't I be friends with Faith and Tia? They're nice."

Izzy rolled her eyes. "Please! Faith is an airhead who only likes to gossip. Tia's no better."

"That's your opinion," Melissa said as they walked out of the candy shop. "I like them."

"When is this party?"

"Next Friday."

"*Next* Friday?" Izzy asked. "Melissa, don't you remember? We were going to have a John Hughes video marathon at my house and watch *Sixteen Candles*, *The Breakfast Club*, *Pretty in Pink*, and *Some Kind of Wonderful*. And we were going to pop popcorn and order in pizzas and Chinese food."

"Nothing was definite, Izzy."

"You mean you're not going to come? You'd rather go to Faith's party?"

Melissa didn't know what to say. She really did want to go to Faith's party. If she skipped it, Faith might think she was blowing her off and never invite her again. This was her chance to make some new friends. Didn't Izzy understand that? And they were always having video marathons. Missing this one wouldn't be a big deal.

"Can't we do it another night?" Melissa asked as they stepped onto an escalator. "I really don't want to miss Faith's party."

"There used to be a time when your friends came first, but I guess that's changed," Izzy huffed. "Suddenly boys and parties are more important to you."

"That's not true," Melissa said, hurt.

"Yes, it is. You're not the same Melissa I became friends with last semester. You're someone else. Someone different who I'm starting to dislike." They reached the second floor and Izzy broke away from Melissa and Celeste. "I'll see you around."

Melissa started to follow after Izzy but Celeste put a hand on her arm. "Let her go, Melissa. She needs to be alone. She won't listen to you."

"But why won't she understand?"

"Don't worry, Melissa. I'll talk to her."

Celeste hurried after Izzy, leaving Melissa alone. Suddenly she felt like she didn't have a friend in the world.

Chapter 8

The Body Connection was Westdale's hottest gym. It was *the* place where twenty-somethings went to work out, as well as students from Westdale University and Westdale High. The lighting was bright and the exercise equipment the most up-to-date. There was an Olympic-sized swimming pool, saunas, Jacuzzis, and an indoor running track. Rock music blared from speakers and the big screen TV sets mounted on the walls were always tuned to MTV, except on Monday nights when the channel was switched to *Melrose Place*.

Melissa had joined The Body Connection at the beginning of the month when she'd returned home from summer camp, wanting to stay trim and in shape. Working out in her own free time was much more fun than gym class at school. Maybe it was because she got to do what she wanted and didn't have to worry about Miss Doynan blowing a whistle in her ear.

Tonight the gym was packed. Everywhere she looked she saw buffed bodies and chiseled muscles.

Melissa was seated on a stationary bike, trying to work up a sweat, but couldn't stop thinking of Izzy and their fight at the mall that afternoon.

Why had Izzy gotten so upset with her? They'd rearranged plans before and it had never been a problem. Just because she wanted to have other friends, it didn't mean she didn't want to be friends with Izzy. Did Izzy think that?

Melissa began pedaling faster, wiping away the beads of perspiration gathering on her forehead.

Her friendship with Izzy meant a lot to her and she'd never do anything to jeopardize it. But her life was changing and she was getting a taste of the popularity she'd always wished for. Now when she walked through the halls, students recognized her. They smiled and talked to her. All she wanted to do was experience it for a little bit.

Still, Izzy's feelings were hurt and Melissa didn't want that. Even though they hadn't specifically said they were going to have a video marathon, they *had* discussed it. And that meant she should have talked with Izzy and Celeste first before accepting Faith's invitation.

What she had to do now was tell Faith she couldn't make her party.

"Hey, Melissa. I didn't know you were a member."

Melissa looked up from the handlebars of her bike and saw Faith standing in front of her. She stopped pedaling and used the white towel around her neck to dry her wet face. "I just joined."

Faith was wearing a hot-pink body suit with a matching headband wrapped around her forehead. She looked perfect, making Melissa feel frumpy in the oversized sweatshirt and shorts she was wearing. Looking around, she noticed a lot of other female exercisers were dressed the same way as Faith. In the future she'd have to remember to dress better when coming to the gym, but how could you look your best when you were all hot and sweaty?

Melissa peeked over Faith's shoulder for her ever-present shadow. "Where's Tia?"

"Tia never works out. She's a couch potato."

"Lucky Tia," Melissa said, hopping off the bike and wiping off the seat according to the gym's rules. "I'm parched. Want to have a drink at the juice bar?"

Five minutes later they were both sipping tall frothy glasses of carrot juice.

"There sure are a lot of cute guys here, aren't there?" Faith said.

Melissa nodded her head while sipping her carrot juice through a straw.

"But that doesn't matter if you're already dating someone," Faith casually added.

Melissa laughed. "You're relentless, you know that?"

"That's why I'm always the first to know," Faith boasted. "So, is it true?"

"Well, Seth and I are going Rollerblading Friday afternoon and to the county fair next Saturday," Melissa answered discreetly.

"It's going to be tough keeping him out of Laurel's clutches," Faith said. "Keep your guard up. She plays dirty."

Melissa didn't doubt that, thinking of the "ghost" she'd seen in the woods the night before.

"Did you know she's a member?" Faith pointed across the gym where Laurel was working out on a StairMaster. She was wearing red spandex shorts and a white T-shirt that bared her midriff. She looked great and a lot of the guys around her were paying more attention to Laurel than their workouts.

Melissa and Laurel made eye contact for a second before Laurel pretended she hadn't seen her and started talking with Zach, who was on the StairMaster next to her. He threw a look Melissa's way also, but like Laurel, ignored her.

Melissa decided she wasn't going to let Laurel and Zach's presence upset her. Let them say whatever they wanted about her. It didn't matter. "Listen, Faith, I wanted to talk to you about your party."

Faith's eyes lit up. "It's going to be a blast," she said excitedly. "I'm so glad you're coming."

"That's just it," Melissa said. "As much I want to come, I can't."

"You can't?" Faith looked disappointed. "How come?"

"You know Izzy and Celeste? I forgot I made plans with them that night."

"No problem," Faith said. "They can come, too."

"You mean it?"

"Sure. Why not? The more the merrier."

"Thanks, Faith. That's awfully nice of you."

Faith finished her carrot juice. "See you later. I'm off to the tanning beds."

"Those machines aren't good for you," Melissa warned.

Faith inspected her image in a wall that was lined with mirrors. "I don't ever use them but now that summer is gone, my tan is fading and I'd like to keep it a few weeks longer. It's just this one time."

"Don't bake yourself too long," Melissa said.

"I won't," Faith promised.

After Melissa left the juice bar she decided to join the aerobics class that was getting ready to start. On her way to the class, she passed Laurel, who was still on the StairMaster, and Zach, who had moved on to bench-pressing weights. She looked around for Betsy, expecting to see her, but she wasn't anywhere in sight.

Twenty minutes later, while Melissa was bouncing to the beat of Janet Jackson's latest hit song, a scream ripped through the gym. The music stopped and a second scream followed, filled with agonizing pain. Melissa froze in place. That voice. It sounded so familiar.

And then she realized why.

It was Faith's.

Rushing out of the aerobics class, Melissa followed a bunch of people to the tanning area at the back of the gym. Because so many people were already there, clustered around the doorway, Melissa couldn't see a thing.

"What happened?" Melissa asked a dark-haired girl wearing purple spandex.

"One of the tanning beds malfunctioned."

"Was anyone hurt?"

"A girl. Someone said it looks like she's been burned on her arms and legs."

Outside the gym Melissa could hear the wail of an ambulance's siren getting closer and closer. Then the doors of the gym burst open and two paramedics wheeling a stretcher hurried through. The crowd of onlookers broke away from the doorway so the paramedics could reach the back of the gym. Melissa tried to catch a glimpse of Faith, but the wall of people instantly closed up.

When the paramedics came back out, they had Faith strapped down on the stretcher underneath a blanket. Her eyes were closed and her face was pale, all traces of her summer tan gone. She was lying so still, Melissa couldn't even see the rise and fall of her chest. Was she breathing? She looked as if she were dead.

"Is she going to be all right?" Melissa asked one of the paramedics.

"It's too soon to tell," he answered, hurrying with the stretcher to the nearest exit. "She's been burned pretty badly. We've got to get her to the hospital."

After the paramedics left, the area with the tanning beds was closed off and people began going back to their exercising.

"Guess I was right," Laurel said.

Melissa whirled around. In all the commotion, she hadn't even noticed Laurel. "What do you mean?"

"About what I said this afternoon. Anything can happen. Who would have thought Faith would have such a horrible accident?"

But was it an accident? Melissa wondered. It seemed too much of a coincidence. And then there was her near fatal accident in the school auditorium. She began wondering again if Laurel could have been behind it. How badly did she want to be Homecoming queen? Could Laurel have done something to the tanning bed?

Standing next to Laurel was Zach, with a twisted smile on his face. His ice-blue eyes locked with Melissa's. "Poor Faith," he said. "I wonder if she'll still be able to compete for Homecoming queen."

Melissa didn't know what to think of Zach's words. They were supposed to be sympathetic, but they didn't sound it. They sounded false, like he really didn't care what happened to Faith. Could he have tampered with the tanning bed to get Faith out of the running? He did want Betsy to win, but how far would he go?

"I guess we'll have to wait for Faith to tell us what happened," Melissa said.

"If she doesn't die first," Zach said.

After a quick shower and change of clothes, Melissa was ready to leave the gym. Once she got home she planned on calling the hospital to see how Faith was doing.

On her way out she was surprised to see Izzy waiting by the registration desk.

"Izzy, what are you doing here?"

Izzy waved a membership application. "I was thinking of joining and decided to pick up a form."

"You were?" Izzy didn't need to join a gym. She had a super high metabolism and could eat whatever she wanted without ever gaining an ounce. Something was up. Izzy seemed very edgy, but what would she have to be edgy about? "Is that the only reason you're here?"

"No," Izzy admitted, fidgeting. "I called your house after dinner and your mom told me you were here. I came to apologize. I was thinking about what happened at the mall today. It was pretty selfish of me not to want you to go to Faith's party."

"No, it wasn't," Melissa said. "I should have checked with you and Celeste before I told Faith I'd go."

"We can have the video marathon another night," Izzy said. "I want you to go to Faith's party."

"I don't know if there's going to be a party."

"Why not?"

"A tanning bed malfunctioned while Faith was using it."

"How awful!" Izzy gasped. "Is she going to be okay?"

"I don't know. She was rushed to the hospital. Didn't you see the ambulance?"

"I just got here."

"She looked awful, Izzy," Melissa whispered. "Like she was dead. She doesn't deserve this. She's so nice. In fact, when I told her I couldn't make it to her party because I'd already made plans with you and Celeste, she told me to invite you guys."

Izzy looked stunned. "She did?"

"What's the matter?" Melissa asked. "You look upset." She took a closer look at Izzy. No, upset wasn't the right word. It was guilty. Izzy looked guilty, but what was she feeling guilty about?

"I'm surprised, that's all," Izzy explained. "It was really nice of Faith to invite Celeste and me. I guess I underestimated her."

Melissa realized Izzy probably felt bad for misjudging Faith. "I told you she was nice, but you didn't want to belive me. I'm going to call the hospital when I get home. It looked pretty bad. I hope she pulls through this."

Izzy echoed Melissa's words. "I hope she pulls through, too."

Chapter 9

Melissa arrived at school early the following morning, desperate to find out about Faith's condition. The hospital wouldn't release any information when she'd called the previous evening and when she'd tried calling Tia, all she'd gotten was a busy signal.

Everywhere she went, students were talking about Faith's accident, but no one knew how she was doing. And even though no one wanted to say it, Melissa could see everyone was thinking the same thing: For all they knew, Faith could be dead.

Melissa's stomach began to grumble and she realized she'd rushed out of the house without having breakfast. She was on her way to the cafeteria when she saw Tia coming in through a side entrance.

"Tia!" she called, racing to her side.

Tia looked up and Melissa could see her

eyes were red from crying. At the sight of Melissa, tears began streaming down Tia's cheeks again.

"How's Faith?" Melissa asked. "The hospital won't tell anybody anything. I tried calling you last night, but the line was busy. Faith's going to be okay, isn't she? She isn't . . ." Melissa couldn't bring herself to finish the sentence, and her stomach knotted up as she waited for Tia's answer.

"No," Tia whispered. "She's not dead. But she came close. She's got third-degree burns on her arms and legs and has to go to a clinic in New York for skin grafts. She's going to be out of school for a long time."

"Do they know what caused the accident?"

Tia shook her head, wiping away her tears. "The health club doesn't have any answers yet, but they're investigating. And Faith doesn't remember anything."

"Want to get some breakfast?" Melissa asked. "I was on my way to the cafeteria."

"I'm not very hungry," Tia admitted. "But I'll sit with you."

Melissa gave her a hug, wishing there was some way to make her feel better. She could see Tia was still thinking about Faith. "She's going to pull through this, Tia," Melissa reassured her.

Tia nodded her head. "I know she is. Faith's a fighter."

Once they reached the cafeteria, students swarmed around Tia, wanting to hear what she knew about Faith. Melissa tried to stay by Tia's side for moral support, but a bunch of Tia's friends from the drama club pulled her over to their table.

"I'll talk to you later," Tia said. "Thanks for listening, Melissa."

"No problem," Melissa said, wishing she could do more.

She headed for the hot food line and ran into Celeste, who was getting French toast.

"I heard about Faith," Celeste said, raising her voice so she could be heard above the clatter of pots and pans crashing around in the kitchen. "Is she going to be okay?"

"Tia told me she has to go to New York for skin grafts," Melissa said, adding a container of milk to her tray.

"Guess you know what that means," Celeste said as they paid a cashier for their breakfasts and walked to an empty table.

"What?" Melissa asked as they sat down.

Celeste opened a container of syrup and drizzled the thick amber liquid over her French toast. "She's out of the running for Homecoming queen."

"I hadn't even thought of that," Melissa said.

"Well, somebody else has."

Celeste pointed with her fork to the blackboard in front of the cafeteria, where the names of each of the five girls running for Homecoming queen were listed. Standing in front of the blackboard was Kimberly. After looking at the five names, she picked up an eraser and wiped away Faith's name.

The rest of the week passed by uneventfully. Melissa's fortune cookies and chocolate kisses were a huge hit and Izzy was busy trying to come up with other ideas. One idea she had was to hand out balloons printed with VOTE FOR MELISSA on them.

Friday afternoon Melissa was standing in front of her closet, trying to decide what to wear for her date with Seth. He'd be arriving in fifteen minutes, so she had to make up her mind fast.

The phone rang and Melissa snatched up the receiver.

"Hi, it's Izzy. Let me guess. You're still standing in front of your closet."

"Help!" Melissa wailed.

"Have you got a pair of faded jeans? A tank top and flannel shirt?" Izzy didn't wait for an answer. "Roll up the sleeves. Put your hair in a ponytail. Go for an all-American look. You can look drop-dead gorgeous the night of the Homecoming dance."

"He hasn't asked me yet," Melissa said, digging through the hangers in her closet for a blue-and-white plaid flannel shirt.

"Why don't *you* ask *him*?" Izzy suggested. "This is the nineties."

"I couldn't."

"Why not?"

Melissa found the shirt she was looking for and pulled it out. "I'll think about it. Look, I've got to go, otherwise I'm never going to be ready."

"Okay. Maybe I'll see you at the park."

"You're going to be there?"

"The Nature Club is. We're planting a butterfly garden."

"I'll keep an eye out for you," Melissa said, pulling a pair of faded jeans out of a dresser drawer. "Is Celeste going to be there, too?"

"She's going to an open house at Westdale University to check out the campus. Oops, gotta go! My ride is here."

Melissa hung up and quickly changed her clothes. She was debating over whether or not she should put on some makeup when the doorbell rang.

"I'm coming," Melissa called, hurrying down the stairs. Pausing before the front door, she took a deep breath and then opened it.

"You look nice," Seth said.

"Thanks." Seth looked terrific in black shorts and a snug white T-shirt. "You don't look so bad yourself," Melissa said.

"Ready to hit the park?"

Melissa stepped onto the front porch and slammed the door behind her, slinging her skates over one shoulder as they headed for Seth's car. "Ready."

Once they got to the park, they geared themselves up. First came the knee pads and then they snapped on their Rollerblades, wrist guards, and helmets.

"Think you'll be able to keep up with me?" Seth asked with a mischievous grin, tightening the helmet strap under his chin.

"Just try to lose me," Melissa said with a grin of her own.

They started down a patch that curved around the park. Mixing with the flow of joggers and bicyclists, they zipped from side to side at a leisurely pace. After twenty minutes of skating, they stopped to get a drink of water from a park fountain.

"You're pretty good," Seth said, wiping at

his mouth with the back of his hand when he'd finished drinking. He stepped aside so Melissa could have her turn at the fountain.

"Thanks," Melissa said, taking a sip.

"There's something I wanted to ask you," Seth said as they headed for a bench under a grove of elm and oak trees.

"What?" Melissa asked, sitting down. The area they were in was shaded, and Melissa enjoyed being out of the sun for a little while.

Seth took off his helmet and tossed his head back, running a hand through his hair. "Are you going to the Homecoming dance?"

"I'll be there because I'm running for Homecoming queen," Melissa answered, trying to keep her voice as even as possible.

"Has anyone asked you to go with them?"

"No."

"Would you go with me?" Seth asked, moving closer and whispering in her ear.

"I'd love to go with you," Melissa whispered back in his ear. And before she could stop herself, she gave him a kiss. On the lips!

Melissa jumped to her feet and pretended the kiss had never taken place. "Come on," she urged.

"Let's race to the lake," Seth suggested, strapping his helmet back on. "Loser has to do whatever the winner wants."

"Like what?" Melissa asked, suddenly suspicious.

"How about another kiss?"

Melissa pretended to consider it. "I suppose I could live with that."

"Ready, set, go!" Seth cried, racing down the path.

Melissa headed after Seth, taking her time to catch up with him. After all, if all he wanted was a kiss, who was she to complain?

Yet when Melissa turned around the curve that lead down to the lake, she was surprised to find Seth standing in the middle of the path.

"We can't go any farther," Seth said, pointing to a yellow sawhorse a few feet ahead of them in the center of the path. "The lake is closed off."

"I wonder why," Melissa mused.

At that moment a park ranger came into sight. Overhearing Melissa's question, he provided an answer.

"We're smoking out the trees around the lake," he explained. "There's an unusually large number of wasp nests and beehives this year. A lot of people have been stung in the last couple of days."

Melissa shuddered. "Ouch!"

"What's the matter, Melissa? Afraid of a little sting?"

Melissa turned around to face Laurel and Betsy, who were on Rollerblades. Both looked sensational in cutoff denim shorts and brightly colored halter tops. Comparing herself to the two, Melissa suddenly felt like one of Cinderella's ugly stepsisters.

"I'm not looking to get stung," Melissa said.

"Then I'd listen to that park ranger and stay away from the lake," Laurel said. "Come on, Betsy. Since the lake is closed, let's head to the other end of the park." Laurel waved good-bye as she skated away with Betsy. "See you guys at school."

Melissa couldn't believe it. She'd been expecting Laurel to somehow ruin her date with Seth, but she hadn't.

A second later there came the sound of a cry from the path Laurel and Betsy had skated around, followed by Betsy's shouts for help.

Melissa and Seth skated down the path. When they came around the curve they found Laurel on the ground with Betsy by her side.

"Laurel, what happened?" Seth asked, concern in his voice.

"I fell," Laurel said. "I think I sprained my ankle." She tried to get to her feet, but couldn't. Tears welled in her eyes. "It hurts."

"Seth, what are we going to do?" Betsy asked. "We walked to the park. I can't get her home."

"Don't worry about it, Betsy," Seth said. "Melissa and I drove. I can take Laurel to the emergency room in my car."

"I don't want to go to the hospital," Laurel quickly said. "Just take me home. My mom can look at it."

"How are we going to get her to your car?" Betsy asked.

"Easy," Seth said, scooping Laurel up off the ground.

Laurel wrapped her arms around Seth's neck, resting her head on his shoulder.

Suddenly, Laurel's tears were gone. The look of pain on her face disappeared and she gave Melissa a crafty smile.

And then it hit Melissa. Laurel was faking!

"Is there going to be enough room in your car, Seth?" Betsy asked. "Laurel's going to have to spread her leg out on the back seat and I'll have to sit in the front. There really aren't supposed to be more than two people in the front seat."

"You're right," Seth agreed.

"Couldn't you walk home, Melissa?" Betsy suggested. "I would walk but no one's home at Laurel's house yet, and I don't want to leave her alone."

"You don't mind walking, do you, Melissa?" Seth asked.

Melissa silently shook her head. What else could she do? If she complained or accused Laurel of faking, it would look like she was jealous.

"Could we go, Seth?" Laurel asked. "My ankle's really starting to hurt."

"I'll call you later, Melissa," Seth promised.

Would he? Melissa wondered. Or would Laurel try to make the most of this moment to win Seth back? They'd gone out for months, while she and Seth had only had one date — and a very short one at that.

Standing by herself, watching as Seth, Laurel, and Betsy disappeared from sight, Melissa realized she'd been right. Laurel *had* ruined her date with Seth.

Chapter 10

"I can't believe Seth fell for that!" Izzy exclaimed. "It's the oldest trick in the book."

"I saw Laurel at the mall this afternoon and she wasn't even limping," Celeste said.

"That doesn't surprise me," Melissa said. "You should have seen her in action, playing the helpless female."

"Isn't this line ever going to move?" Celeste moaned, checking the time on her watch. "The movie's going to start soon, and I don't want to miss a minute of *The Strangler!*"

"It's in 3-D," Izzy raved. "You'll actually be able to see his hands coming off the screen. Like they're wrapping around your neck!"

Melissa made a face. "Ugh!" She hated horror movies, but *The Strangler* was her treat as a way of making things up to Izzy and Celeste.

"Did Seth call you last night?" Izzy asked as the line began moving.

"No," Melissa whispered.

"Something probably came up," Izzy said reassuringly.

"You think so?"

"Seth's crazy about you, Melissa. He asked you to the Homecoming dance! I don't think he's fallen back into Laurel's clutches."

"So what'd you guys do today?" Celeste asked.

"I bought a really great slip-dress that I'm going to wear to the Homecoming dance," Izzy said. "It was a real steal, only ten dollars."

Celeste turned to Melissa. "How about you?"

Melissa sighed. "I just waited for Seth *not* to call."

"He's going to call, Mel," Izzy said. "Mark my words."

Was Izzy right? Melissa didn't want to think the worst, but ever since yesterday afternoon, her imagination had been out of control. She kept seeing Seth begging Laurel to take him back.

After finally buying their tickets, they got some snacks and headed into the theater to find seats.

Five minutes later they were still looking.

"I can't believe there aren't three seats to-gether," Izzy complained, gazing around the crowded theater.

"We'd better hurry," Celeste urged. "The lights will be going down soon."

"Let's face it," Melissa pointed out. "We're not going to be able to sit together. I'm going to sit in the balcony."

After dividing up their snacks, Melissa hur-ried to an empty seat in the balcony and slipped on her 3-D glasses. A second later the lights went out and eerie music began filling the dark-ened theater.

Melissa didn't like sitting by herself. She wished Seth was sitting next to her. He'd wrap his arm around her and she'd bury her eyes against his shoulder, peeking at the screen only when she thought it was safe.

The music ended and heavy breathing filled the theater, growing stronger and stronger. Soon it sounded as if it were right in Melissa's ear. She squirmed uncomfortably in her seat, reminding herself that the movie wasn't real.

A teenage girl appeared on the screen, run-ning into an empty house. She dashed for the phone, frantically calling for help, but no one was answering her cries. A second later she realized why. The phone line was dead.

Then a sinister voice whispered, "I'm going to kill you, Melissa. You can't get away from me."

Melissa practically jumped out of her seat before she realized the name of the girl on the screen was Melissa.

The girl dropped the phone and ran into another room, slamming the door shut and locking it. She began backing away from the door. As she did, she moved closer and closer to a window covered with drapes. As she drew closer to the window, the drapes began to move and a pair of hands reached out, wrapping around the girl's neck.

The girl on the screen fought for her life, struggling to tear the hands away. She couldn't breathe!

Suddenly Melissa had trouble breathing, too.

It was as if the 3-D hands emerging from the movie screen were actually squeezing her own neck, digging into her skin.

And then she realized the awful truth.

There *were* a pair of hands wrapped around her own neck!

And a voice whispering in her ear.

"It's time to die," the voice crooned. "It's time to die."

Chapter 11

Melissa screamed.

Someone was strangling her!

"Help!" Melissa yelled, batting at the hands around her neck, sinking her nails into the skin. "Help me!"

The lights in the theater instantly came on and the movie on the screen stopped running. The hands around her neck disappeared and Melissa turned around in her seat, to face a blond-haired teenage guy she'd never seen before.

"What's your problem?" she shouted.

"Sorry," he said, his cheeks turning red with embarrassment. "I thought you were my girl-friend. I guess I sat down in the wrong row. I was coming back from the candy counter and thought I'd scare her. I was only playing a joke."

Izzy and Celeste hurried to Melissa's seat.

"Some joke!" Izzy snapped. "You nearly scared her to death."

The blond-haired guy apologized again and headed for an empty seat two rows behind Melissa. He slunk down into the seat next to his girlfriend, who gave him a nasty look.

Now that the mystery had been solved, the audience tore their eyes away from Melissa and back to the screen.

"Are you okay?" Izzy asked.

"I'm fine," Melissa said, rubbing a hand around her sore neck. "But I'm going to head home."

"We'll go with you," Celeste said.

"No," Melissa insisted. "Stay and enjoy the movie. You were looking forward to it."

"Are you sure?"

"Positive." She couldn't even think of watching the rest of the movie.

The first thing Melissa did when she got home was turn on all the lights. Then she made sure all the windows and doors were locked. And though she hated herself for doing it, she went from closet to closet, checking to make sure no one was hiding inside.

Melissa knew she was being silly, but she was home alone. Her parents wouldn't be back until after midnight and the little bit of the movie she'd seen had creeped her out. She even checked the phone to make sure it was working.

When she was finished inspecting the house, Melissa settled down on the couch with a magazine, Salt and Pepper curled up at her feet. She'd hardly begun reading when the phone rang.

Melissa glanced at the grandfather clock in the corner of the living room while picking up the phone. It couldn't be Izzy or Celeste because the movie was still playing. Maybe it was Seth.

"Hello," Melissa said, eagerly waiting to hear Seth's voice.

No one answered.

"Hello? Is anyone there?"

Still no answer. Only the sound of heavy breathing.

Like in the movie.

Melissa scolded herself for letting her imagination run away with her. It was probably just a crank call. She started to hang up but then heard a voice on the other end of the line.

"Melissa . . ."

Melissa's blood turned to ice.

"Melissa, are you there?"

"I'm here," Melissa whispered, not knowing

how she managed to speak. The voice on the other end of the line sounded like the voice of pure evil.

"You're being bad, Melissa. Very bad. And bad girls have to be punished. Like Faith was punished."

"Who is this?" Melissa demanded. "What's your name?"

"It's Brenda, Melissa. Brenda Sheldon . . ."

Melissa gasped and the line went dead.

"It had to be Laurel," Izzy insisted the following evening when Melissa called and told her about the call from the previous night. "Who else could it be? She wants you to drop out of the running for Homecoming queen and she's trying to scare you."

"Do you really think so?"

"Who else could it be?" Izzy laughed. "You don't think it's Brenda Sheldon calling from beyond the grave, do you?"

Melissa didn't know how to answer. Ghosts didn't exist. Spirits didn't return from the dead. But what if they were wrong? What if in some unexplainable way Brenda Sheldon was having her revenge against the girls running for Homecoming queen because she felt no one else deserved to wear the crown?

"What about Faith's accident?" Melissa asked.

"That's all it was," Izzy said. "An accident."

"I wish I wasn't running for queen," Melissa confessed. "As much as I like all the attention, I'm starting to get scared. I think I might drop out of the running."

"No!" Izzy exploded. "You can't do that!"

"Why not?"

"Because it's exactly what Laurel wants you to do! What are you? A quitter?"

"No," Melissa answered.

"Then don't drop out. Nothing's going to happen to you, Melissa. Trust me."

Before Melissa could say anything else, Izzy started talking about the movie and how scary it was. Melissa could hear Izzy's mother in the background, demanding Izzy let her use the phone.

"Guess I'd better hang up. Hey, did Seth ever call?"

"Yes. This morning. He had to go out of town Friday night for the weekend. Yesterday was his grandfather's seventy-fifth birthday and there was a party."

"See!" Izzy gloated. "I told you he hadn't fallen into Laurel's clutches!"

Melissa chuckled. "Yes, Izzy, you were

right. *Again.* I'll see you at school tomorrow."

After getting off the phone with Izzy, Melissa headed down to the dining room to set the table. Her parents had gone out to get a pizza and would be returning home soon.

Melissa was in the middle of folding napkins when the doorbell rang. With Salt and Pepper trailing behind her, she opened the front door, surprised to find a long rectangular-shaped box tied with a red ribbon on the doorstep.

Melissa looked around, expecting to see a delivery man, but no one was in sight.

"I wonder what this could be," she mused, picking up the box and carrying it into the kitchen.

Buried underneath the ribbon was a card. Tearing it away, she saw it had her name written on it. Putting the box down on the kitchen table, she undid the ribbon and lifted the lid.

Nestled inside the box were mounds of white tissue paper. It had to be flowers from Seth. How romantic!

Pushing aside the tissue paper, Melissa expected to find a beautiful bouquet. But the smile on her face quickly disappeared when she saw what was really inside.

It was a bouquet of dead roses tied with a black ribbon.

With trembling fingers, Melissa opened the card that had been attached to the box, reading the message inside:

ROSES ARE RED
VIOLETS ARE BLUE
THESE FLOWERS ARE DEAD
AND SOON YOU WILL BE, TOO

Chapter 12

"I don't think this is a good idea, Izzy."

"Why not?" Izzy turned around and the bright glare of the flashlight in her hand caused Melissa to squint and look away. "You said you wanted to see Brenda Sheldon's grave. You said you wanted to make sure she was dead and buried."

"I know," Melissa admitted, shivering as a cold burst of wind cut through the denim jacket she was wearing. "But couldn't we come back during the day?" She gazed around the dark and deserted cemetery. "It's creepy here at night."

"After we've come all this way?" Izzy huffed. "Don't you think it's a little late to change your mind?"

"Let's just get this over with," Melissa said, looking up at the cloudy sky. Thick, dark clouds filled the air, ominously rumbling. "It looks like a storm is going to start."

"We've only got a little bit farther to go," Izzy said, continuing on.

"I should have stayed home with Celeste," Melissa grumbled as she hurried after Izzy, keeping her eyes straight ahead. She tried to ignore the tombstones on either side of her, and the shadows they created.

An ominous feeling of dread seeped through Melissa's bones. She felt the same way she had last night when she'd received the bouquet of dead flowers and read the card attached to them. After her parents had come home from the pizzeria, they'd called the police, but the officers who'd come to her house hadn't taken her very seriously. A practical joke was what they called it.

But Melissa knew it was no joke. Someone had wanted to scare her. Would the person stop with just a scare, or would he — or she — try to kill her?

Melissa looked around the cemetery again, unable to shake the fear that had gripped her. Something was wrong. Someone was out there, waiting, watching.

"Let's go home, Izzy." Melissa tugged on her arm. "I don't want to do this."

"Wait! I think this is it," Izzy announced, stopping in front of a marble tombstone. She aimed her flashlight at the letters engraved in the stone.

"You're right," Melissa whispered as Brenda Sheldon's name was revealed, along with the dates of her birth and death.

The flashlight began to flicker and Izzy turned it off, immersing them in total darkness.

Melissa clutched Izzy's arm. "Why'd you do that?" she asked, afraid. It was pitch-black and she was unable to see anything. "Turn it back on!"

"I don't want the batteries to go dead," Izzy explained, shaking off Melissa's grip. "We need to see where we're going when we leave. Come on, let's take a closer look and then we'll go."

As Melissa's eyes adjusted to the darkness and they neared the tombstone, she could see it hadn't been cared for in years. The corners were crumbling and there were cracks in the marble, spreading from one end to the other. The grass surrounding the grave was dry and brown, choked with weeds and clusters of dead flowers.

"It doesn't look like anyone's been here in ages," Melissa whispered. "That's so sad. It's like everyone's forgotten she ever existed."

Suddenly Melissa was glad for the flowers

she had brought along. Nothing fancy, just some daisies. She knelt down, wiping away the dead flowers and pulling up weeds.

"Want to give me a hand, Izzy?"

Melissa waited for Izzy to kneel down beside her, but she didn't.

"Izzy?"

When she still didn't get an answer, Melissa looked over her shoulder and gasped.

Izzy was gone.

"Izzy?" Melissa called out. "Izzy, where are you?"

She jumped to her feet and looked frantically around the deserted cemetery. Where was Izzy? She didn't know how to make her way back to the main gate and she didn't have a flashlight. She couldn't stay in the cemetery all night!

"This isn't funny, Izzy," she called out, trying not to panic. "If you're trying to scare me, it's not going to work."

A clap of thunder burst through the dark sky and fat drops of rain began to fall. Melissa started to get wet and she realized she was going to have to find shelter somewhere and then try to find a way out on her own.

Still clutching the daisies she'd brought along, Melissa knelt back down to place them on Brenda's grave. At that moment a jagged flash of lightning ripped through the sky, illuminating the night.

It also illuminated the decomposing hand reaching out from Brenda's grave, clamping around Melissa's wrists and pulling her down toward the opening grave.

Melissa screamed and struggled to break free, but the grip was like iron. She was powerless to escape.

A figure began emerging from the ground.

Grass and soil began breaking away as the decomposing body of Brenda Sheldon revealed itself. She was wearing her torn and tattered Homecoming gown, streaked with mud.

Melissa's eyes darted around the cemetery. All around her, other graves began rupturing open as the living dead began climbing out.

Heading for Melissa.

She struggled to escape, but it was useless.

The skeleton's mouth opened and an evil cackle emerged. Empty cavities where eyes had once been were now possessed by a dull red glow, and they burned into Melissa.

"It's time for you to be crowned queen, Melissa," Brenda screeched. "Queen of the Dead!"

"No!" Melissa shouted. "No!"

Wide-eyed, Melissa sprang up in bed, her

heart beating rapidly. Her eyes darted from corner to corner, expecting to see a corpse reaching out to grab her. Instead, all she saw were the familiar sights of her bedroom: the rocking chair in the corner, the chest at the foot of her bed, the bookcase and television stand.

As they came more into focus, Melissa began to calm down. She was home. She was safe. Nothing could hurt her. It had only been a dream.

The numbers of her alarm clock glowed 2:15. Drenched with sweat, Melissa changed into a new nightshirt and then went to the bathroom for a drink of water. On the way back to her room she stopped outside her parents' bedroom, listening to the reassuring sound of her father's snores. Just knowing her parents were on the other side of the door made her feel safer.

Back in her bedroom, Melissa went to the windows and pulled the curtains closed. Then she slid back under the sheets with Salt and Pepper curled at the foot of her bed.

The nightmare she'd had was still vivid in her mind, and Melissa tried hard to forget it. She kept reminding herself that it had only been a dream. Her parents were right down the hall. No one could get her.

Reassured, Melissa closed her eyes and didn't open them until the following morning when her mother started knocking loudly on her closed bedroom door.

"Melissa, wake up. This is the third time I'm knocking. It's eight o'clock. You're going to be late for school."

At the sound of her mother's voice, a groggy Melissa jumped out of bed and quickly dressed. She didn't bother with breakfast, trying to save time, but it didn't matter. When she finally arrived at school, the second bell had already rung.

Melissa's first class of the day was gym and she hurried to the girls' locker room. Once there she changed out of her clothes into a pair of shorts and a T-shirt. Not bothering to lock her locker, she hurried into the gym.

Attendance was still being taken and Melissa rushed to take her place in line behind Tia, answering when her name was called. After attendance was taken, Miss Doynan had the class start doing jumping jacks, followed by sit-ups and push-ups.

"Why doesn't Miss Doynan get with it?" Tia groaned as she struggled to finish her sit-ups. "The other gym teachers do step aerobics and Jazzercise. Sit-ups and push-ups are so boring."

Melissa agreed. For her the class was even more boring because Izzy and Celeste weren't in it.

After Tia finished her sit-ups, Miss Doynan blew her whistle and announced that the class would be playing volleyball. Melissa groaned. She hated volleyball. There was no way to hide or run from the ball like you could do in basketball and touch football. If the ball came directly at you, you had to hit it. And if you missed, you had to deal with angry teammates who blamed you for screwing up.

Melissa and Tia ended up on the same team with Betsy, who was a fierce volleyball player. Each time Melissa made a mistake or failed to make a proper serve, Betsy was all over her.

"What's her problem?" Tia asked when she and Melissa rotated positions.

"She wants to win," Melissa said, keeping her eyes on the net. "And not just at volleyball."

Tia shook her head. "I don't get girls like Betsy. What's wrong with just having fun and a good time? Winning isn't everything."

"It is to her," Melissa said, wondering if Betsy was the one who had sent her the bouquet of dead flowers.

Finally, after a grueling thirty-minute game, Miss Doynan blew her whistle and class was over. While Betsy stayed behind to high-five the rest of their teammates for winning, Melissa hurried for the showers.

On the way back to her locker, Melissa ran into Laurel, who was changing into shorts and a T-shirt for the second period gym class. Other girls were arriving to change their clothes while girls from Melissa's class were leaving.

"Hi, Melissa. Ready for today's vote? You've had the lead for a week. Think you can keep it?"

Before Melissa could answer Laurel, Tia came rushing up to her. "Melissa, could I borrow your psychology textbook? I left mine at home and you know what a crankcase Sajecki is. I'll get it back to you before fourth period. Promise."

"No problem," Melissa said. She finished toweling her hair dry and pulled it into a loose ponytail. "My locker's open. I didn't have time to lock it before class. Just take it."

"Thanks," Tia said.

While Tia went off to her locker, Melissa turned her attention back to Laurel, wondering what to say. Laurel was acting friendly, but that was probably all it was: an act.

"How was your weekend?" Laurel asked. "Anything exciting happen?"

What was that supposed to mean? Was Laurel expecting her to tell her about the phone call on Saturday night? Or the flowers she'd received last night? Had she been the one to send them? She wouldn't put it past her.

Just then there was a loud scream.

"Help me!" Tia screamed. "Somebody help me!"

Melissa whirled around with the rest of the gym class and gasped.

She couldn't believe what she was seeing.

Tia was fighting off a mass of bees swarming out of Melissa's open locker.

Chapter 13

Melissa wanted to help Tia, but she didn't know what to do. She stared at the bees swarming out of her locker as one thought kept repeating itself in her mind: *That could have been me. If I had opened my locker, I would have been the one getting stung by those bees.*

There were so many bees. It was like a dark tornado was blowing out of Melissa's locker and wrapping itself around Tia. Stinging her over and over.

Melissa could hear someone shouting for help, but no one was coming to Tia's rescue. Pandemonium had broken out in the locker room. Girls were screaming, rushing for the nearest exits. Not wanting to get stung, they were shoving and kicking each other so they could be the first to get away.

The commotion finally caused Miss Doynan to come out of her office. As soon as she saw what was happening, she raced to Tia. Ignoring the bees that had now turned their attention on her, she slammed the locker shut, trapping most of them inside.

"It hurts," Tia cried. "It hurts."

"I know," Miss Doynan said in a soothing tone of voice. "I know. But we're going to get you to a hospital. Everything's going to be fine, Tia."

Melissa watched as Miss Doynan hurried Tia out of the locker room. Her face was already swelling from the stings she'd received.

"Poor Tia," Laurel said. "If she hadn't asked to borrow your book, this never would have happened to her."

"It would have happened to *me*," Melissa said, turning to face Laurel. "That's what was supposed to happen, wasn't it? You were the one who put those bees in my locker."

"What?!" Betsy exclaimed, overhearing Melissa and instantly coming to Laurel's defense. "Are you crazy?"

"Where would I get bees to put in your locker?" Laurel asked.

"From the park," Melissa said. "You were there Friday when the ranger on duty was telling Seth and me about the beehives by the lake."

"Why would Laurel do something like that?" Betsy demanded.

"To send me a warning," Melissa said. "So I would drop out of the competition. It wouldn't have been hard to put the bees in my locker. Laurel was all by herself in the locker room while we were taking our showers."

"You were by yourself, too," Betsy reminded.

Melissa was confused. "What are you talking about?"

"You were the last one to class," Betsy said. "No one was around. Who's to say you didn't plant those bees in your locker so Tia would get stung?"

"That makes no sense. Why would I do something like that?" Melissa demanded.

"For the same reason you accused Laurel of doing it," Betsy stated. "To get rid of the competition. At the same time, you throw suspicion off yourself. Everyone thinks you were supposed to get stung, when all along, it was really Tia."

"How was I supposed to know Tia would ask to borrow my psychology book?" Melissa shot back.

"You didn't. If she hadn't asked, you would have found some reason for her to open your locker," Betsy explained.

"That makes sense to me," Laurel said.

"I'll bet it'll make sense to everyone else, too," Betsy agreed.

"You can't go around spreading a story like that," Melissa said. "It isn't true."

Betsy shrugged. "Some students will believe it and some won't. The only way we'll know for sure is when it comes time to vote for Homecoming queen."

When Melissa arrived in the cafeteria at lunchtime, everyone stared at her. She knew it wasn't because she was still wearing her T-shirt and shorts from gym class. Her locker, with her clothes still inside, had been taken away after being fumigated through a vent.

Everyone was staring because of Laurel and Betsy.

They'd started spreading their rumor.

The first thing Melissa wanted to do was run away. But if she were to do that, it would look like she was guilty, and she wasn't. She hadn't done anything wrong. How could they believe she'd do such a thing to Tia?

Melissa scanned the cafeteria, looking for a friendly face. It would be so much easier to take a step inside if she knew someone was on her side. But no one smiled at her. After all the clubs and committees she'd joined, no one waved her over to their table.

Wendy Morgan and Nancy Pederson from the Fine Arts Committee looked the other way. Lisa Jackson, Natalie Bishop, and Matt Crose from the Spanish Club pretended not to see her. Jessica Gregory and Julian Biddle, who were on the Dance Committee, stared right through her.

Realizing she'd been standing in the doorway for too long, Melissa headed for an empty table at the back of the cafeteria. Conversations stopped as she walked by and students looked at her suspiciously, whispering into each other's ears.

Things got better by the time she reached her table. A few girls from the Board Games Club had made eye contact with her and smiled, and Izzy was coming off the hot food line. There was no mistaking her in the v-neck paisley dress and sandals she was wearing.

Catching sight of Melissa, Izzy hurried over and took the seat opposite her.

"I heard what happened in gym class," Izzy said. "Are you okay?"

"I'm fine," Melissa answered, no longer feeling alone. "What did you hear?"

"Everything. Including the lies Laurel and Betsy are spreading."

"You don't believe them, do you?" Melissa whispered.

"Of course not!" Izzy exclaimed. "I could kill them for what they're doing. Talk about playing dirty! But we've got to do damage control, Mel. This could cost you votes."

"I don't care about votes. I just want people to believe I didn't do it."

"I believe you," a voice behind Melissa said.

Melissa turned around in her seat and saw Seth. Standing next to him was Celeste.

"Me, too," Celeste added.

Melissa gave them both a smile. "Thanks."

Seth took the chair next to Melissa, wrapping a consoling arm around her shoulders. "How are you doing?"

"Much better now," Melissa said. "I wish I was wearing my clothes, but they had to fumigate my locker."

"Has anyone heard how Tia is?" Celeste asked.

"She's still at the hospital," Izzy said, opening a bag of barbecue potato chips and offering them around the table. "They're giving her antihistamines and plan on keeping her a couple of days for observation. She'll probably be back sometime next week."

"Who could have done such a horrible thing?" Celeste asked.

"It was Laurel," Melissa answered. "She'll do anything to become Homecoming queen. First, there was the falling sandbag that nearly hit me, then Faith's accident at the health spa, and now this. Every time something's happened, she's been there."

"I agree with you, Mel," Izzy said, "but you want to hear something crazy?" Izzy leaned across the table. "I heard some girls outside the library saying that the Homecoming competition is jinxed, that Brenda Sheldon has cursed it because she's jealous and doesn't want anyone else wearing her crown."

Celeste looked up from the sandwich she was unwrapping. "What's so crazy about that? I've heard it."

"So have I," Melissa said.

"Let's look beyond Brenda Sheldon and Laurel," Seth suggested, popping open a can of soda. "Who else could have done it?"

"Not Betsy," Melissa said. "She was in class with everyone else when I arrived late."

"I saw Zach Kincaid hanging around the girls' locker room on my way to second period," Celeste said. "He could have been waiting for Betsy to get out of class . . ."

" . . . or he could have put the bees in Melissa's locker," Izzy finished.

"That makes sense," Melissa agreed. "He does want Betsy to win."

"Hey, Kimberly is posting this week's Homecoming queen results," Izzy said, standing up on her chair and watching as the student council president moved from column to column. She let out a squeal of delight and shook two fists in the air when Kimberly was finished. "Melissa, you're still in the lead!"

"What's the rest of the listing?" Celeste asked.

"You're not going to believe it," Izzy said.

"Tell us," Celeste urged. "Don't keep us in suspense."

"Betsy's in second place."

"What about Laurel and Tia?"

"Third and fourth. By the way, Seth," Izzy added, "you're still in the lead for Homecoming king."

"Congratulations, Melissa," Celeste said, giving her a hug. "Only one more week to go! You're going to win. I just know it."

"What's the matter, Melissa?" Seth asked when she didn't say anything. "Why so quiet? You're still in the lead."

"I can't stop thinking about Tia," Melissa said. "Seth, *I* was the one who was supposed to get stung by those bees. What if the person who put them in my locker decides to try something else?"

"I won't let them," Seth promised.

He gave Melissa a reassuring hug, but it didn't help. She was scared. Accidents kept happening to the girls running for Homecoming queen. Could Laurel be the one behind it all? Zach? Betsy? Could it even be Brenda Sheldon?

No matter who it was, the competition was becoming deadly.

Chapter 14

"Are you having a good time?" Seth asked.

"The best," Melissa answered. "Want some cotton candy?"

"I'll stick to peanuts," Seth said, tossing one in the air and catching it in his mouth.

Melissa stuck out her tongue. "Show-off."

"You're just mad because you can't do it. How many times did you try before? Ten? Twelve?"

"Fifteen," Melissa grumbled. "At least I made the squirrels happy. I left them a feast."

"How 'bout I win you a stuffed animal," Seth said, reaching into his jeans for a dollar bill as they approached a ring toss.

It took Seth five more dollars, but he finally managed to toss his ring over a square cube.

"Which do you want?" Seth asked when it came time to pick out a prize.

"That one," Melissa said, pointing to a white teddy bear with a red ribbon around his neck.

Melissa cuddled the teddy bear after Seth handed it to her. "He's so adorable. I'm going to name him Ted, for Teddy bear."

Seth rolled his eyes. "Whatever you say."

Melissa kissed Seth's cheek. "Thank you."

"For what?"

"Tonight. I'm having a lot of fun. You've helped me forget how awful things have been lately."

"It hasn't been that bad," Seth said. "Nothing else happened this week."

"You're right," Melissa admitted. And then she asked the question she was afraid to ask. "But will it last?"

After the incident with the bees, the rest of the week had passed by uneventfully. No phone calls. No mysterious packages. No accidents. It was almost too good to be true. It was the way her life used to be before she decided to run for Homecoming queen.

Thankfully, after Monday, Laurel and Betsy's gossip had been ignored and no one was whispering behind her back. But the way she'd been made to feel like an outcast had been frightening; it made her realize she didn't want to be in the spotlight anymore. She wanted to blend in with everyone else. That way, when she did make a mistake, she wouldn't feel like the whole world was watching.

"You shouldn't worry about things that might never happen," Seth said. "Whoever it was, Principal Phelps threw a scare into them at Monday's special assembly."

"For now," Melissa said. "But the threat of police involvement isn't going to scare that person for very long."

And then that person will be back, Melissa thought, shivering. *Ready to strike again.*

"Are you cold?" Seth took off his letterman jacket and wrapped it around Melissa's shoulders.

The heavy bulk of the navy blue jacket warmed Melissa against the cool night breeze. "Thanks."

"That looks pretty good on you. Why don't you keep it?"

Melissa traced a finger over the white *W* on the left hand side of the jacket. "You mean it?"

"Uh-huh. Unless you don't want it."

"No! I want it," Melissa rushed to answer. "I'd love to wear your jacket." She gave Seth a shy smile. "This is the first time a guy's ever given me anything that belonged to him."

Seth took Melissa's hand in his. "Come on. Let's have some fun."

They spent the rest of the night going from ride to ride. First the Tilt-A-Whirl, then the roller coaster and merry-go-round. After that they went on the Ferris wheel and rode the bumper cars.

The best part of the night came when they took a ride in the tunnel of love. At first, all Seth did was hold Melissa close as their swan boat floated in the darkness. Then, as the ride drew to an end and the heart-shaped exit neared, he lifted her face toward his and gently kissed her on the lips.

It was the perfect kiss.

Once they were back on the fairgrounds, Seth wrapped an arm around Melissa's waist, pulling her close to him as they walked. Having Seth hold her this way made Melissa feel like they were a real couple. It left her with a warm, cozy feeling inside and she couldn't ever remember having had such a wonderful night out.

Not even bumping into Laurel, Zach, and Betsy had spoiled things. It had been a tense few minutes, especially when Laurel had seen Melissa was wearing Seth's letterman jacket — her eyes had practically popped out of her head. Yet instead of starting a fight, Laurel had walked away with Zach and Betsy, not saying a word.

"What do you want to do next?" Seth asked.

"I don't care," Melissa said, pulled out of her thoughts. She squeezed Seth's arm affectionately. "What do you want to do?"

"Hey, look!" he exclaimed excitedly. "A haunted house. I love haunted houses."

Melissa followed Seth's finger to the gloomy building he was pointing at. It was two stories, with shuttered windows, thick strands of ivy climbing up the stone front, and dilapidated steps leading to a rickety porch. Sneering gargoyles lined the rooftop and jack-o'-lanterns with sinister smiles rested on the windowsills.

"Let's go inside," Seth said, eagerly hurrying up the steps.

The last thing Melissa wanted to do was go into a haunted house, but she could see Seth really wanted to. "Okay," she said, trying to sound enthusiastic.

"You just made it," the ticket seller said as he handed Seth two tickets. "No more customers after this. Take your time. You've got the whole place to yourselves."

Melissa stuck close to Seth's side as they stepped into the house and started walking down a long hallway. The inside was dark and it took a while to adjust to the dim lighting. As they did, they saw cobwebs hanging from the ceiling and tiny red eyes glowing underneath the furniture they passed.

"Rats," Melissa whispered when she heard tiny squeaks. "They're not real, are they?"

"Of course not," Seth said.

Although she was reassured by Seth's answer, Melissa kept away from the furniture. She was afraid one of the rats might turn out to be real.

When they reached the end of the hallway, a closed coffin was spread out before them. Organ music was playing in the background, followed by the cackling shrieks of a witch. As they walked by, the coffin lid opened and a screaming skeleton popped out. Startled, Melissa jumped, grabbing Seth's arm as the coffin lid slammed shut.

It was more of the same as they went from the living room, where "ghosts" floated in the air, to the dining room, where a decomposing family of corpses sat around the skeletal remains of a turkey.

"This is really lame," Seth snorted. "Let's check out the upstairs."

Most of the second floor was identical to the first, with some exceptions. In one bedroom a pair of hairy arms with yellowed claws reached out from underneath a bed while in the bathroom a sinister voice coming from the drain in the bathtub sang, "the phantom's gonna getcha . . . the phantom's gonna getcha."

"Let's get out of here," Melissa said, covering her ears. She hated the sound of the voice and didn't want to hear it anymore. It was the kind of voice you heard in your nightmares, coming closer and closer, until you woke up screaming.

The next room they walked into had mirrors lining all the walls. But these mirrors weren't like regular mirrors. Each one provided a completely different reflection. In one mirror Melissa could see she was tall and skinny; in another she looked short and fat.

"Now this is cool," Seth said, rushing from mirror to mirror and staring at distorted images of himself.

"Seth, don't get too far ahead," Melissa said as he left her side.

"Don't worry," he teased, disappearing into another room. "The phantom's not gonna getcha."

"Seth, I don't want to be alone," Melissa said, hurrying after him. "Wait for me."

The room Melissa walked into was filled with shroud-covered furniture. She looked around for Seth, but he was nowhere to be seen. Was he hiding behind one of the pieces of furniture, waiting for her to pass by so he could jump out and scare her?

Melissa took cautious steps farther into the room. "Seth? Seth, where are you?"

Other than the creaking of her footsteps on the floorboards, she heard nothing. Outside the windows, the wind was howling through the eaves of the roof. But then, as she listened more closely, she started to hear a low, raspy voice.

"The phantom's gonna getcha . . . the phantom's gonna getcha."

Melissa's blood froze and her eyes darted around the dark room, trying to pinpoint where the voice was coming from.

"Stop it, Seth," she called out. "This isn't funny."

But the chanting only continued. Getting louder and louder.

"The phantom's gonna GETCHA. THE PHANTOM'S GONNA GETCHA. THE PHANTOM'S GONNA GETCHA . . . AND THEN HE'S GONNA KILL YA!"

Those last words caused Melissa to bolt from the room. Suddenly scared, all she wanted to do was get to the hallway, down the stairs and back outside.

It had to be part of the haunted house, she

kept telling herself. That's all it was. It wasn't Seth. He wouldn't do something this mean to her.

She hurried back into the room filled with mirrors. As she raced through the room, she noticed something. Something that was impossible. She had to be wrong. Her eyes were playing tricks on her.

She stopped in her tracks.

All remained still.

Except for one dark shape that was coming closer and closer.

Melissa didn't want to turn around, but knew she had to. She had to see what was standing behind her.

Slowly, she twisted her body around.

And screamed.

Standing a few inches away from her was a figure dressed in black from head to toe. A ski mask was pulled over the person's face. All she could see was the person's eyes.

They were cold.

Hard.

Glittering with hatred.

"Who are you?" Melissa asked.

"I'm the phantom," a low, raspy voice growled.

"What do you want?" Melissa asked, trying to keep her voice from trembling. *This is only make-believe*, she told herself. *Only make-believe. It's part of the haunted house. That's all it is.*

"I want to kill you," the phantom answered, lifting up an ax.

Run! her mind screamed. *Run! This isn't part of the haunted house. This is for real!*

But before Melissa could even move, the phantom lifted the ax and swung with a piercing shriek.

Melissa ducked her head and fell to the floor as the ax crashed into the mirror behind her. Shattered glass scattered around her as she struggled to her feet, dropping her teddy bear while the phantom pulled the ax free from the mirror and swung a second time.

This time the ax landed on the floor with a dull thud, missing Melissa, but chopping off the head of her teddy bear.

The phantom picked up Ted's head and waved it at Melissa, cackling madly. Then the phantom tossed it to one side and lunged at Melissa.

Melissa ran to the door at the end of the room, but when she tried to twist the knob, it wouldn't open. Abandoning the locked door, Melissa looked around desperately for another exit, but there was nowhere to go.

She was trapped!

Melissa started pounding frantically on the walls, screaming for help until she was hoarse. Yet no one came to her rescue. Her screams blended in with the prerecorded screams of the haunted house. No one knew she was in danger!

Behind her she could hear the footsteps of the phantom getting closer and closer, the chant getting louder and louder.

"The phantom's gonna getcha. The phantom's GONNA GETCHA. THE PHANTOM'S GONNA GETCHA!"

Then something happened as she pounded on a wall. First, there was a whirring sound. Then, as she clung to the wall, it began to twist and turn.

The next thing Melissa knew, she was in another room.

And the phantom was on the other side of the wall.

She was safe. Safe!

But her relief was short-lived. Through the wall she could hear shrieks of anger and outrage. After that she began to hear pounding on the wall.

The phantom was trying to find the button she'd accidentally pressed! She had to get out of the room before the wall started to turn again.

Melissa ran from the room and out into the hallway. Spying a staircase, she hurried down it, looking over her shoulder to make sure she wasn't being followed. Twice she nearly tripped, grabbing onto the banister in the nick of time.

Back on the first floor she ran in the direction of the nearest exit, thrusting through the door.

"Where've you been?" Seth asked as she raced down the front steps. "I've been waiting fifteen minutes. Did you find one of the secret exits? I was leaning against a wall and all of a sudden I was flying down a laundry chute. I landed in the basement on a foam mattress. It was wild!"

Melissa collapsed into Seth's arms. "The phantom," she sobbed. "The phantom tried to kill me."

"Melissa, calm down. What's wrong? What happened?" Seth gripped her by the shoulders. "You're trembling. Why are you so upset?"

Trying to catch her breath, she told Seth what had happened to her in the haunted house.

"Melissa, you're overreacting," Seth said when she was finished.

"No, I'm not," she cried, pointing back to the house. "He's inside with an ax. He tried to chop my head off. He tried to kill me!"

"You *think* he was trying to kill you," Seth explained, "but he really wasn't. He was trying to scare you, that's all. It was part of the haunted house."

"No, it wasn't," Melissa insisted. "I can tell the difference between what's real and fake."

Seth took Melissa's hand in his. "I'll prove it to you. Let's go find the ticket seller. He'll tell you I'm right."

But when they went to find the ticket seller, he was nowhere around.

"Want me to go inside and take a look?" Seth asked, starting to climb the steps. "Maybe someone's closing things up."

"No!" Melissa shouted, clutching his arm. What if Seth went inside and didn't come back out? What if the phantom was waiting for him? "I don't want you to go in there."

"No one's going to hurt me, Melissa." Seth gave her a hug. "Or you. Come on. Let's go home."

"But it seemed so real," Melissa said, looking back at the house as they started walking to the parking lot.

"That's why you got so scared and overreacted. You forgot that it was fake."

As they walked away, Melissa looked over her shoulder and stared at an upstairs window.

The lace curtains that were hanging started to move, slowly being drawn back.

It's the wind, Melissa told herself. *Only the wind.*

But was it? Afraid she'd see the same black-hooded face that had stalked her earlier, Melissa turned her back on the house, pressing herself closer to Seth.

She was silent during the drive home. Was Seth right? Was it all part of the haunted house? She wanted to believe it. She would have believed it. Except for three things:

Laurel.

Betsy.

Zach.

The three of them had been at the fair tonight. One of them could have been the one in the haunted house, looking to eliminate her from the Homecoming race.

Permanently.

It was after midnight when Melissa finally got to bed. Salt and Pepper were sleeping in their usual spot at the foot of her bed. Melissa had just nestled under the covers and was drifting off to sleep, remembering the kiss Seth had given her when he'd walked her to the front door, when her cordless phone rang.

Not wanting to wake up her parents, she

stumbled out of bed and hurried over to her dresser to answer it.

"Hello?" she whispered sleepily.

First there was silence at the other end of the line, then a soft, low voice whispered, *"Almost lost your head tonight, Melissa. That would have been awful. A queen can't wear her crown without her head."*

The sound of the sinister voice jolted Melissa awake. All traces of sleep were gone. It was the voice from the haunted house!

"Who is this?" Melissa finally demanded when she was able to speak. "Why are you doing this to me?"

But there was no answer. The line was dead.

Chapter 15

Monday was the final day of voting for the Homecoming queen and Melissa was a nervous wreck.

The thought of eating made her stomach queasy, so she skipped breakfast. She messed up a pop quiz in American history because she couldn't concentrate and she almost dropped a beaker in anatomy because her palms wouldn't stop sweating.

After what seemed like an eternity, lunch arrived, much to her relief. By the end of the hour the suspense would be over and she'd know if she had won or lost.

"This is it!" Izzy squealed excitedly when Melissa sat next to her. "The day we've been waiting for!"

"We don't know for sure if Melissa's going to win," Celeste reminded, peeling a banana.

"How can she not win? She's been in the lead for two weeks."

"How was your weekend?" Celeste asked, biting into her banana. "Did you and Seth have fun at the fair?"

Melissa hadn't had a chance to talk to either Izzy or Celeste on Sunday. She'd been too busy telling the police what had happened in the haunted house and about the phone call she'd received Saturday night.

It turned out the masked person with the ax *hadn't* been part of the haunted house. The police had learned that when they'd gone to the fair and talked to the person running the haunted house.

But the police weren't worried. Detective Caruso, who was overseeing the case, told Melissa and her parents that in all likelihood, someone was playing a practical joke on her, like with the flowers. After all, Halloween was just around the corner.

Melissa's parents were satisfied with Detective Caruso's answers, but Melissa wasn't. Once again, the police had acted like she was wasting their time. What was it going to take to have them take her seriously? Her body?

"It went fine," she answered.

"That's it? Just fine?" Celeste had a disappointed look on her face. "Nothing romantic happened?"

"We kissed," Melissa admitted. "A couple of times."

Izzy shushed Melissa and Celeste. "We can talk about your hot date later. Kimberly's going to announce the winner."

Looking across at the next table, Melissa could see Laurel and Betsy sitting on the edge of their seats, eyes glued on Kimberly. Zach was sitting next to Betsy, an arm draped around one shoulder, whispering in her ear. She gave him a smile, then turned her gaze back to Kimberly.

"The moment you've all been waiting for has finally arrived," Kimberly announced. "First, I want to thank everyone for giving so generously with their votes. We raised a lot of money to help Westdale High."

Hoots and yells filled the cafeteria. When they died down, Kimberly continued. "I have in my hand the name of Westdale High's new Homecoming queen. As I'm sure you're all aware, this is our first Homecoming queen in twenty-five years. Before I announce the name of the winner, why don't Melissa, Laurel, and Betsy come on up so we can give them a big round of applause."

As students began clapping and cheering, Melissa followed Laurel and Betsy to the front of the cafeteria. Seth gave her a wink and a thumbs-up when she passed his table.

"I know you're all dying of suspense," Kimberly said as Melissa, Laurel, and Betsy stood behind her. "So here it is." She paused dramatically and looked at the list in her hand. "Westdale High's new Homecoming queen is Betsy Sullivan."

Betsy screamed and threw her arms around Laurel, jumping up and down, while Melissa stood numbly next to them.

She'd lost. She wasn't going to be Westdale High's Homecoming queen. She'd known all along there was a possibility she might lose. But deep down, in the secret part of herself she kept hidden from the rest of the world, she'd been sure she was going to win. Everyone had been rooting for her. Everyone had been *voting* for her.

Across the cafeteria she could see Zach being slapped on the back by his buddies. Celeste had a sympathetic look on her face, but Izzy was nowhere around.

Melissa was disappointed, there was no denying that, but in a way she was also relieved.

The competition for Homecoming queen

was over. Maybe now her life would get back to normal.

After her last class, Melissa headed to the auditorium to practice for the Homecoming ceremony. She, Laurel, and Tia would be Homecoming princesses to Betsy, kind of a consolation prize for not being crowned queen. They'd be escorted by Homecoming princes, the three guys who had lost out to Seth, who was voted Homecoming king. The crowning ceremony would take place Saturday afternoon at halftime during Westdale's first football game against North Ridge High, and the Homecoming dance would be later that night.

The last place Melissa wanted to be was around Betsy. It wasn't that she was a sore loser, but she knew Betsy was going to gloat and rub things in. Sure enough, she did.

"I told you that you weren't going to win, Melissa, but you didn't want to believe me," Betsy said sweetly, sitting on her throne. She was surrounded by a bunch of her girlfriends from the cheerleading squad, who were all making a big fuss. "I'll bet you were really disappointed when Kimberly announced my name. I guess you'll think twice the next time you try to compete with someone like me."

"Come try on your robe, Betsy," Laurel said, holding out a red velvet robe trimmed with white fur.

Watching Betsy slip into her robe and crown, Melissa couldn't help but feel a pang of jealousy.

"Don't let her get to you," Seth whispered in her ear.

Melissa turned to Seth and smiled. "When did you get here?"

"A couple of minutes ago. Coach kept us late after basketball practice."

"How's it feel to be Homecoming king?"

"It'd be a lot more fun if you were my queen."

"You're a sweetie."

"I'm sorry you lost," Seth said. "How about a movie tonight? You look like you need some cheering up."

"I can't. Our washing machine broke and I promised my mom I'd go to the Laundromat."

"Why don't I come along and help?" Seth offered.

"Thanks, but I'd really like to be by myself."

Seth shrugged. "If that's what you want."

"Okay, people, let's get started," Miss Doynan called, clapping her hands together as she walked down the center aisle of the auditorium. "I need the Homecoming queen and king front and center, with the Homecoming court standing behind them."

As Seth started to walk away, Melissa grabbed him by the arm. She sensed she had somehow hurt his feelings and that was the last thing she wanted to do. "Please don't be mad at me. I love being with you, but right now, I'm feeling sorry for myself and I don't want to be around anyone. You do understand, don't you?"

Seth sighed and ran a hand through his hair. "I'm trying to. But listen, Melissa, I don't care that you're not Homecoming queen. You're still number one with me. That's all that should matter, don't you think?"

Melissa nodded her head, realizing how lucky she was. Suddenly, losing didn't seem to matter as much. "I think you're absolutely right."

Practice lasted over an hour. Miss Doynan was a perfectionist who kept having them do things over and over until she was satisfied. Each Homecoming princess had to walk in with her prince. Once they reached the stage, they had to stand behind the king and queen's thrones. Then, when Betsy and Seth were seated, the crowns and robes were brought out. First, Betsy was crowned by one of the princesses. Then it was Seth's turn.

As luck would have it, Melissa, because she came in second place, was the one who got to crown Betsy.

"Make sure you don't mess my hair," Betsy hissed under her breath when Melissa placed the crown on her head.

Melissa ignored the remark and placed the crown gently, keeping a smile on her face. But by the fifth time she had to crown Betsy, after listening to one complaint after another, she was ready to smash the crown over her head.

Finally Miss Doynan let them go, reminding them that there would be another rehearsal Wednesday afternoon and one on Friday when Tia returned to school.

"Want a ride home?" Seth offered as they walked off the stage.

"Let me grab my jacket out of my locker and I'll meet you in the parking lot," Melissa said.

As Melissa walked through the hallways, she could see a few after-school activities were still going on, including the Recycling Club. As she passed by the classroom where they were having their meeting, Izzy caught sight of her and raced out.

"What happened to you?" Melissa asked. "You disappeared at lunch."

Izzy gave Melissa a guilty look. "I didn't mean to desert you, but I couldn't bear to stick around and watch that witch gloat over winning."

Melissa twisted the combination lock on her locker and snapped it open. "Well, it's over." She reached into her locker for her jacket. "The best thing to do is forget about it."

Izzy pounded a fist into the locker next to Melissa's. The sound of clanging metal filled the quiet hallway. "I can't forget about it! She didn't deserve to win, Melissa. You did! I said you were going to become Homecoming queen and I let you down."

Melissa had never seen Izzy so angry before. "Izzy, you didn't let me down. We all tried our best. There's nothing you can do."

A sly, calculating look appeared on Izzy's face. "Want to bet?"

A feeling of panic gripped Melissa. "What are you going to do?"

"You'll see," Izzy stated mysteriously. "You'll see."

"Izzy, please don't do anything you're going to regret," Melissa begged. "It's not worth it."

"I'm not going to regret anything," Izzy said. "*Betsy* is."

Melissa watched Izzy stomp down the hallway. Worried about what she might do, Melissa slammed her locker shut and hurried after her. But when she reached the end of the hallway, Izzy was gone.

Just then, Celeste was coming up the stairs.

"Did you see Izzy?" Melissa asked.

"No. Why?"

"She was acting really weird and I think she's going to do something she shouldn't."

"Does this have to do with Homecoming queen?" Celeste asked.

Melissa nodded her head. "In a way. Izzy was really freaked out over Betsy winning. I've never seen her so angry."

Celeste looked around the deserted hallway and then moved closer to Melissa. "If I tell you something, you've got to swear you won't breathe a word to Izzy."

"I swear," Melissa promised.

"I hate myself for even saying this," Celeste said, an anguished look on her face, "but I think she's the one behind all the accidents."

"What?!" Melissa exclaimed. "Why would you say something like that?"

Celeste reached into the back of the notebook she was carrying and handed Melissa a newspaper clipping. "Take a look at this."

The clipping was from the school newspaper, *The Westdale Word*. It was an article about Homecoming and the five girls competing for queen. Accompanying the article were photographs of each of the girls. A red *X* was marked on all of the faces except Melissa's.

"Where did you get this?" Melissa asked, shocked.

"It fell out of Izzy's history book when she raced out of the cafeteria at lunch."

"It doesn't prove anything," Melissa said.

"I know, but I'm worried. You know how much she hates Laurel and Betsy. She told them you were going to be Homecoming queen and you lost. They're having the last laugh on her again. It must be driving her crazy."

"But we know Izzy. She wouldn't go that far," Melissa insisted, not wanting to believe the worst of her best friend. "She wouldn't hurt anybody."

"How do we know?" Celeste asked. "It freaked her out when you became friends with Faith and Tia. Who's to say she didn't decide to get even with them?"

Melissa didn't want to admit it to herself, but Celeste was right. After all, Izzy was at her health club the night of Faith's accident. And she had acted guilty. At the time she had thought it was because Izzy had misjudged Faith, but could Izzy have tampered with the tanning bed?

"What about the bees in my locker?" Melissa pointed out. "Even though Izzy's gym class is right after mine, why would she do that to me? Why would she try to hurt me?"

"I don't know," Celeste said. "She was at the park the same day as you, so she could have gotten the bees. But it doesn't make sense. Unless she wanted to get back at you for being friends with Faith and Tia."

Could Celeste be right? Could Izzy be the one behind everything? But that would also mean she had made those phone calls, sent her the dead flowers, and tried to attack her in the haunted house.

Melissa didn't want to believe it. Izzy was her friend — she would never do such horrible things.

"What are we going to do, Melissa?" Celeste asked worriedly, on the brink of tears.

"I don't know," Melissa said. "Look, Seth is waiting for me and I've got to head to the Laundromat after dinner. I'll call you tonight. Around nine. We'll figure out something."

After leaving Celeste, Melissa hurried outside and headed for the student parking lot. As she made her way through the rows of parked cars, she could hear two angry voices. As she listened more closely, she recognized them as belonging to Zach and Betsy. Not wanting to be seen, Melissa pressed herself against the side of a white van.

"What do you mean you're breaking up with me?" Zach demanded. "You can't break up with me. Not after everything I did for you."

Betsy laughed cruelly. "Oh, poor Zach. Do you really think I needed you to become Homecoming queen?"

"If it wasn't for me, you wouldn't have won."

Melisssa could hear Betsy's approaching footsteps and started edging toward the rear of the van. But then the footsteps stopped.

"Let go of my arm, Zach. You're hurting me."

"You're not breaking up with me, Betsy. I won't let you."

"Don't tell me what to do!" Betsy shouted. "You've been bossing me around for two years and I'm sick of it."

"I'm warning you, Betsy. If you break up with me, you're going to regret it."

They shouted at each other for a few more seconds until Betsy broke free of Zach's grasp and ran across the student parking lot. An engine then started and Zach pulled out in his car, driving after Betsy.

As Melissa hurried to Seth's car, Zach's words burned in her mind: *You can't break up with me. Not after everything I did for you. If it wasn't for me, you wouldn't have won.*

What did Zach mean?

How far had he gone?

And what exactly did he do?

Chapter 16

After Seth dropped her off, Melissa spent the rest of the afternoon studying. She tried not to think of the conversation she overheard between Zach and Betsy, or her suspicions about Izzy, and focused on her psychology notes. Tomorrow she was having an exam and really wanted to ace it, but no matter how hard she tried, her mind kept wandering.

At around six she started to get hungry and ordered in a pizza. Except for Salt and Pepper sitting by her feet, meowing pitifully until she tossed them each a mushroom slice, she ate by herself because her parents were competing in a bridge tournament and wouldn't be home until after ten.

When she finished eating, she cleaned up the kitchen, took out the garbage, and carried a laundry basket filled with dirty clothes out to her car. She also took along her psychology textbook and notes, figuring she could study while waiting for the clothes to wash.

The streets of Westdale were dark and deserted as she drove to the Laundromat. No one was outside — it was as if everyone had disappeared. Suddenly she remembered a horror movie where aliens invaded a small town. The teenage heroine of the movie, the last survivor of the alien invasion, was alone in her car, trying to drive out of the town. She kept looking nervously in her rearview mirror, watching to see if she was being followed.

When she didn't see anyone behind her and crossed over the town limits, she stopped looking over her shoulder and relaxed.

It was then that the green-scaled alien who had been lurking in the backseat of her car jumped up and grabbed her, sinking his fangs into her neck as her car swerved off the road.

Spooked out by thoughts of the movie, Melissa waited until she reached a red light and quickly locked all the car doors. Then she peeked into the backseat and looked in her rearview mirror before the light turned green.

No one was in the backseat and no one was behind her.

As she drove past the light, a black sedan pulled out from a supermarket parking lot and started driving behind her. The bright glare of the sedan's headlights burned into the interior of her car.

For the next ten minutes, the sedan remained behind her. Melissa found it strange that the sedan wasn't passing her, since it was a four-lane road.

At one point the sedan pulled up beside her and they drove side by side. Melissa tried to get a look into the other car, but the windows were tinted, so she was unable to see who was behind the wheel.

Finally a turn in the road appeared and the sedan veered off to the left. Once the car disappeared from sight, Melissa relaxed her grip on the steering wheel. She didn't know why, but she'd been unnerved by the sedan driving so closely next to her. She'd almost been expecting it to slam into the side of the car, trying to push her off the road. She didn't know why, but there had been something *odd* about the black sedan. It had reminded her of a hearse.

It was eight o'clock when Melissa arrived at the Laundromat, an hour before closing. The parking lot was empty and she found a spot right near the front door.

The inside of the Laundromat was just as empty as the parking lot. A weary-looking mother with two little boys fighting over a red lollipop was at a folding table, dividing her clothes into piles, while a bearded man wearing a Westdale University sweatshirt was unloading a dryer.

Melissa headed for two washing machines, loading whites in one and colors in the other. By the time she had measured out the proper amounts of liquid detergent and bleach for each machine, the two little boys and their mother were gone and the bearded man was walking out the door.

She was all alone.

Lately, it seemed whenever she was alone, something creepy happened.

Melissa pushed the thought out of her mind. Nothing was going to happen tonight. So what if the Laundromat was deserted? The attendant — who made change and checked on the machines when there was a problem — was probably on a break. And there was still an hour before closing. There'd be other people arriving to do their laundry.

Determined to make the best use of her time, Melissa opened up her psychology textbook and started reading the highlighted passages.

Twenty minutes later when the washing machines stopped sloshing, Melissa put down her textbook and transferred her wet clothes into a dryer. After loading them into the machine she tossed in a dryer sheet and set the timer.

Once the clothes were tumbling around and around, Melissa decided to go to the deli down the block. She was thirsty and wanted something cold to drink.

After buying a container of orange juice, Melissa stopped to play a video game. By the time she had finished battling intergalactic space warriors, her clothes were ready to come out of the dryer and she rushed back to the Laundromat.

The first thing Melissa noticed when she got back to the Laundromat was that the attendant still hadn't returned and no one else had arrived to do their laundry.

Her dryer's timer was buzzing loudly and Melissa hurried to turn it off. At home she often helped her mother with the laundry, and there was nothing she loved more than freshly washed clothes coming out of the dryer.

Opening the dryer door, Melissa stuck her hand inside, expecting to feel a warm pile of laundry.

Instead, her hand landed on something wet and sticky.

Confused, Melissa reached deeper into the dryer.

Her fingers hit something round and solid, with long strands attached to it.

Wrapping her fingers around the strands, Melissa started pulling it out of the dryer, wondering what it could be.

When her hand emerged and Melissa saw what she was holding, she stared at it in disbelief.

It was a severed head.

Chapter 17

Melissa screamed, dropping the head to the floor.

It bounced once, then twice, before rolling away.

Suddenly, she heard laughter.

Cruel, taunting laughter.

"You should have seen the look on your face!" Laurel hooted, coming out from behind a washing machine at the end of the Laundromat. "It was priceless."

"We should have set up a video camera," Betsy laughed, emerging from behind another machine. "Then we could have showed everyone at school."

The "head" had stopped rolling and Betsy picked it up by the hair, shaking it at Melissa. "What's the matter?" she asked meanly. "Scare you?"

Now that she'd calmed down, Melissa could

see the "head" Betsy was holding wasn't real, but fake. It was from a mannequin, and they'd covered parts of it with red paint to make her think it was blood.

It was a trick. Another horrible trick.

Melissa's fear evaporated instantly, replaced by blinding anger. She was sick of being the brunt of Laurel and Betsy's twisted jokes.

"Let's see how funny you think this is," Melissa said. Reaching for a bottle of liquid detergent, she twisted off the cap and splashed the front of Betsy's denim jacket.

"Look what you did!" Betsy fumed. "Now I'm going to have to wash my jacket."

"Can't you even take a joke?" Laurel demanded, dabbing at Betsy's wet jacket with a towel.

"You think that was funny? It was sick! You nearly gave me a heart attack," Melissa said.

Spying her laundry piled up in a basket under the folding table, Melissa picked up the basket and stormed out of the Laundromat.

Halfway home, Melissa realized she'd left her psychology notes and textbook at the Laundromat. She slammed the steering wheel in frustration. She didn't want to see Laurel and Betsy again, but she needed her books. She still had more studying to do and couldn't afford to fail tomorrow's test.

Sighing, Melissa turned her car around and headed back to the Laundromat. Hopefully, by the time she got there, Laurel and Betsy would be gone.

Much to her relief, Laurel and Betsy were nowhere around. She found her books where she'd left them on top of the dryer and tucked them under her arm.

As she started walking back toward the exit, the lights in the Laundromat began flickering.

Then they went out, immersing her in total darkness.

Melissa's first instinct was to run, but she forced herself not to. The floor of the Laundromat was made of linoleum and very slick. When she'd come in, she'd noticed puddles on the floor from some of the leaky machines.

Melissa started walking slowly with her hands held out in front of her, feeling her way like a blind person. She tried to adjust her eyes to the darkness, but couldn't see a thing. If anything the darkness seemed to be growing, wrapping itself around her like a thick blanket, getting tighter and tighter until she couldn't breathe.

Melissa started taking larger steps. All she wanted to do was escape the darkness, but in her rush to get outside, Melissa slipped. Before she could fall to the floor, she grabbed at the handle of a dryer.

As she grabbed the door, it popped open and she heard a thud.

It sounded like something had fallen out.

Just then the Laundromat lights came back on. As Melissa's eyes adjusted to the returning light, she saw what had fallen out of the dryer.

It was Betsy, hanging halfway out of the machine.

Her eyes were closed and she wasn't moving.

At first Melissa thought it was another joke. Laurel and Betsy had probably noticed that she had left her books behind. Figuring she'd return to get them, they'd decided to get back at her.

But then she saw the note pinned to the front of Betsy's blouse. There was only one sentence: THE ONLY GOOD QUEEN IS A DEAD QUEEN.

Reading the words, Melissa's blood turned cold and she began backing away from the body in horror.

This was no joke.

Betsy was dead.

Chapter 18

"So what was it like finding a dead body?" Izzy asked, dipping her finger into a bowl of chocolate-chip cookie dough.

"Gross!" Celeste exclaimed, busy spooning cookie dough onto a baking sheet. "Who wants to know that?"

Melissa checked the oven temperature. "Do we have to talk about this?"

It was the day after Betsy's murder and Melissa, Celeste, and Izzy were spending the afternoon baking cookies. Classes had been canceled and would resume the next day. Not wanting to be home alone, Melissa had called Izzy and Celeste, asking them to come over.

"We don't have to talk about it," Celeste said, finishing with her baking sheet and handing it to Melissa, who slid it into the oven. "You know what I heard? Homecoming weekend might be canceled."

"Canceled? How come?" Izzy asked.

"Because of Betsy. It wouldn't be right to have Homecoming weekend when the Homecoming queen is dead!"

"That's what they have runner-ups for," Izzy pointed out. "I'll bet Melissa becomes Westdale's new Homecoming queen."

Melissa was stunned. The thought that she might now become Homecoming queen had never entered her mind.

"And why shouldn't we talk about the murder?" Izzy asked, heading to the refrigerator with Salt and Pepper following after her. They waited patiently while Izzy poured herself a glass of milk and then poured some into their bowl. "There's a killer on the loose, and he might strike again."

"How do you know that?" Melissa asked. "Maybe the killer won't strike again. Maybe whoever killed Betsy had a grudge against her. She upset a lot of people."

Izzy reached for a cookie from a cooling tray. "Like who?"

"Zach Kincaid," Celeste answered, handing Melissa another baking sheet. "They broke up yesterday and there's a rumor going around that he murdered Betsy because he was upset over losing her. If he couldn't have her, no one else could."

"Uh-oh," Izzy said, putting down her cookie and cupping her right eye. "I think my contact is coming out. I'll be right back."

Izzy left the kitchen to go to the bathroom and Melissa began filling the sink with dirty bowls and spoons.

"What was it like talking to the police?" Celeste asked, putting the flour and brown sugar back into a cupboard.

"They took a statement from me," Melissa said, filling the sink with hot water and adding a squirt of Ivory. "They asked me to explain how I found the body."

"Did they ask you anything else?"

"Like who I thought might have killed her?" Melissa asked, dipping her hands into the sudsy water.

Celeste nodded her head. "Yes. What'd you tell them?"

Melissa reached for a sponge and started washing a bowl. "I told them about the fight I overheard between Zach and Betsy. How he told her she'd regret breaking up with him. And I mentioned the accidents that happened to me, Faith, and Tia."

Celeste looked over her shoulder and lowered her voice. "Did you say anything about Izzy?"

Melissa shook her head. "No, but I've been

thinking about things since we talked yesterday."

"Like what?"

"Did you know Izzy was at the gym the night of Faith's accident?"

"No," Celeste gasped.

"I ran into her at the registration desk. She said she was picking up a membership application, but she was acting strange."

"You don't think . . ."

"And she was at the park the day the rangers were getting rid of those beehives."

"Melissa, are you saying Izzy was behind Faith and Tia's accidents? That you think she murdered Betsy?"

Before Melissa could answer Celeste's question, a harsh voice filled the kitchen. "Aren't you going to answer, Melissa?"

Melissa and Celeste turned around. Standing in the kitchen doorway was Izzy, who had overheard most of their conversation. On her face was a look of hurt and disbelief.

"How could you think I'd do such horrible things?" Izzy asked.

"You wanted me to become Homecoming queen," Melissa whispered. "You were determined to see me win."

"That's because you're my friend. I'd do anything for a friend, but I would never hurt anyone. How could you think I murdered Betsy?"

"You hated her, didn't you?"

"That doesn't mean I killed her."

"You were pretty angry at her yesterday afternoon," Melissa pointed out. "You said you were going to do something she would regret. And when she and Laurel were spreading those rumors about me, you said you could kill them."

"I was going to pull a joke on her," Izzy exploded, throwing her hands up in the air. "Something embarrassing. That's it." Izzy shook her head. "Why am I even wasting my breath? You don't believe me. I can see it in your eyes."

"I want to believe you, Izzy. I do," Melissa said. "But so many things have happened. I don't know what to believe anymore."

Izzy grabbed her black motorcycle jacket off the back of a kitchen chair. "You should believe me when I tell you I didn't do anything. Friendship is based on honesty and trust and it's obvious we don't have that anymore. Don't bother calling me, Melissa. Our friendship is over."

After shrugging into her jacket, Izzy slammed out the back door.

"I feel awful," Celeste said. "We really hurt

her feelings, but, Melissa, I have to tell you something."

Melissa tore her eyes away from the back door and looked at Celeste. "What?"

"Last night I called Izzy's house at nine. She wasn't home, but her mother said she'd gone to the library at seven and wouldn't be home until ten. After I hung up I went to the library and looked for her. I didn't see her anywhere and asked Mrs. Babcock, the librarian, if Izzy had left." Celeste's voice rose. "Melissa, Mrs. Babcock was there the entire night and said Izzy never showed up. You know what this means, don't you?"

"Izzy doesn't have an alibi," Melissa whispered in shock.

"Just because she wasn't where she was supposed to be doesn't mean she murdered Betsy," Celeste quickly added.

"I know that," Melissa said. "But if she wasn't at the library, where was she?"

After Celeste went home with a plate of cookies, Melissa finished cleaning the kitchen. She had just filled the cookie jar when the doorbell rang. Wiping her hands on a dish towel, Melissa hurried to answer it. When she opened the door, she was surprised to see Zach on her doorstep.

Melissa's first instinct was to slam the door shut. Zach scared her and she didn't want to be alone with him. But before she could even get the door halfway closed, he shoved it open and took a step inside.

"What do you want?" she asked, trying not to be intimidated by Zach's hulking body. "I didn't invite you in."

"Too bad. The police brought me in for questioning. They heard about my fight with Betsy."

"I only told them the truth," Melissa said defensively. "I only told them what *you* said."

"I didn't kill Betsy and I can prove it," he said. "Last night I was working out at the gym. Plenty of people saw me."

"You might have an alibi for Betsy's murder, but that doesn't mean you weren't behind Faith and Tia's accidents," Melissa said. "Or the things that happened to me. You were willing to do anything for Betsy."

"The only thing I did was get my buddies on the football and baseball teams to vote for Betsy. And they got their friends and girl-friends to vote for her, too."

"Is that the only reason you came over? To tell me you're innocent?"

Zach's ice-blue eyes darkened. "No. I came

to give you a message." He jabbed a finger at Melissa. "I won't forget the way you got me in trouble with the police. When you least expect it, I'm going to get even. Count on it."

Chapter 19

"Are you sure I look okay?" Melissa asked, staring at her image in a mirror.

The hairstylist standing behind Melissa's chair gave her hair an extra spritz of hair spray. "You look gorgeous," she raved. "Just like a Homecoming queen should."

Listening to the stylist's words, Melissa still couldn't believe it. *Homecoming queen.* She was Westdale High's new Homecoming queen.

It still seemed so unreal.

It all started at a special assembly the day classes resumed. First, there was a memorial service for Betsy. Then Principal Phelps announced that Homecoming weekend wouldn't be canceled, but would be held in honor of Betsy's memory.

He also announced that Melissa would be Westdale High's new Homecoming queen.

There was a round of applause after the

announcement was made, but it wasn't very strong. Staring at the faces of the students sitting next to her, Melissa could see some of them looking at her strangely. She didn't know why until the assembly was over and she heard whispering behind her back.

"Is she crazy? The Homecoming court is jinxed. If she wears the crown, she'll die!"

The rest of the week Melissa heard more of the same superstitious whispers. A lot of students were spooked and felt that Brenda Sheldon was reaching out from beyond the grave to curse the new Homecoming queen.

"You couldn't pay me a million dollars to wear that crown," Melissa overheard one girl say to another. "It'd be like signing my own death certificate."

Her friend nodded and ran a finger across her throat. "Ffft!"

Although the whispering she heard about Brenda made her feel uneasy, Melissa tried to ignore it. She kept reminding herself that Brenda Sheldon wasn't a vengeful spirit.

Brenda was dead and buried and couldn't hurt anyone.

But there was other talk, too. Meaner and more malicious. Some students were saying that she was the one behind Faith and Tia's accidents. They were also saying that she had killed Betsy so she could become Homecoming queen.

Melissa knew Laurel and Zach were spreading those rumors. They'd point at her whenever she passed them in the hallways and whisper to whomever they were with. She knew they were doing it on purpose. Zach had promised to get even with her for talking with the police and Laurel couldn't stand that Melissa was Homecoming queen.

It was hard to ignore their words. Tears would burn at the back of her eyes, but she refused to cry. She had always wanted to be the center of attention, but not this way. When she decided to run for Homecoming queen, she thought she'd get the chance to see what it was like to be popular, to have everyone want to be her friend. But in the weeks since she'd been running for Homecoming queen, she'd learned a valuable lesson.

It didn't matter how many parties you were invited to, how many clubs you belonged to, or how many boyfriends you had. What mattered most was having friends who liked you for who you were, friends who were there when you needed them.

Like Izzy and Celeste.

Celeste was the perfect friend, always ready to listen, help out, and offer advice. Izzy was the same way, but Melissa didn't know if Izzy would ever speak to her again. She hadn't seen her the rest of the week because she was out sick with a cold, but whenever she called Izzy's house, Izzy refused to take her calls. And when the police announced they were looking to question a drifter who'd disappeared the night of Betsy's murder, Melissa felt even worse. Even though there had been a cloud of suspicion surrounding Izzy, she should have given her the benefit of the doubt.

"Why so sad?" the hairstylist asked, removing the hot-pink smock covering Melissa. "Today should be one of the happiest days of your life."

"I was thinking of how I hurt a friend," Melissa said, getting out of the chair and taking another look at herself in the mirror.

Because everyone's eyes would be on her today as she was being crowned, Melissa had splurged on a morning of beauty at the local salon. Besides a facial, manicure, and pedicure, she'd also had her hair washed and styled.

She wasn't the only one getting the full treatment this Saturday morning. Everywhere she looked in the salon there were girls from Westdale High getting their hair or nails done for the Homecoming dance. She recognized a few faces, but no one smiled or asked her to join them. They were all treating her like an outsider.

Anxious to leave the salon, Melissa hurried to the cash register. She had just finished paying her bill when Laurel walked in with one of her friends from the cheerleading squad. When she saw Melissa, the smile on her face disappeared.

"Bet you can't wait to be crowned Homecoming queen this afternoon," Laurel said, raising her voice so she could be heard by the other girls. All eyes in the salon turned to Laurel and Melissa, waiting to see what would happen next. "But don't forget that the only reason you're Homecoming queen is because Betsy is dead."

Melissa didn't bother answering. She headed for the front door of the salon and pulled it open. As she started to step outside, she bumped into Tia, who was entering.

It was the first time Melissa had seen Tia since she was stung and most of the swelling on her face had gone down. She'd be returning to school on Monday, and would be part of the Homecoming court today.

"Hi, Tia. Sorry I bumped into you. I wasn't

watching where I was going," Melissa apologized. "How are you feeling? Did you get the card I sent?"

"Sorry, I can't talk," Tia said, brushing past Melissa. "I'm late for my appointment."

Melissa stared after Tia in stunned disbelief. She'd thought Tia was her friend, but even she was giving her the cold shoulder.

"Guess you're not wanted here," Laurel said smugly.

Melissa didn't know what to say. What could she say? For once, Laurel was right.

The big moment finally arrived at three o'clock. Like the rest of Westdale High, Melissa, Seth, and the Homecoming court were at the football field. They were sitting in the first row of bleachers, watching the Westdale Wildcats trounce North Ridge High. So far the score was 28 to 3.

The bleachers were packed with students and alumni waving blue and white banners emblazoned with huge *W*s and cheering loudly. Directly across from the bleachers a platform had been set up for the Homecoming ceremony, decorated for autumn with orange and gold streamers, pumpkins, leaves, and dried husks of corn. Already sitting on the platform was Principal Phelps, Miss Doynan, and a few other members of the faculty.

"I can't wait until this is all over," Melissa confessed to Seth.

"How come?" he asked.

"I'm afraid something is going to happen."

"Like what?"

"I don't know. Maybe another accident."

"Relax." Seth squeezed Melissa's hand reassuringly. "It's only stage fright."

When halftime arrived, Principal Phelps stepped up to the microphone in the center of the platform. After welcoming back the alumni, he began announcing the names of the Homecoming court. Tia and her partner walked up to the platform first, followed by Laurel and her partner.

Then it was Seth and Melissa's turn.

Principal Phelps's voice boomed loudly through the outdoor speaker system. "It's my honor to present Westdale High's new Homecoming king and queen, our first in twenty-five years. Let's all give a big round of applause to Seth Powell and Melissa Brady."

"This is it," Seth said, clasping Melissa's hand in his.

The school band started playing as Melissa and Seth rose from their seats and walked up the platform steps. When they reached Principal Phelps, they each shook his hand before slipping into the red velvet robes that were held out for them. Once the robes were on, they were handed their scepters.

It was time to be crowned.

Melissa was first. Because she was so nervous, she closed her eyes and held her breath as Laurel placed the crown on her head. It felt heavier than she remembered at rehearsal and she lifted a hand to prevent it from sliding off her head. Butterflies danced in her stomach as she kept waiting for something to happen. But the sky didn't suddenly darken. The platform didn't collapse.

Nothing happened.

Melissa opened her eyes and smiled at Seth, who was already wearing his crown. Then she took his hand in hers and together they faced the bleachers, waving.

The Homecoming court remained on the platform for the rest of the football game and watched Westdale win its first game of the season. After it was finished, they posed for yearbook pictures, as well as for photos for the school newspaper and the local paper. Melissa smiled and said "Cheese" over and over until she thought her face would crack.

Finally after the last picture was taken and the last question asked, Melissa was allowed to leave. As she weaved her way through a crowd of well-wishers, she found Celeste waiting for her.

"You look great, Melissa," Celeste said, giving her a hug. "Very queenly."

"Thanks, Celeste." Melissa hugged her back. "It means a lot having you here today."

"I wouldn't have missed it for the world."

Melissa looked around hopefully. "Did Izzy come?"

"No, she didn't."

"Oh," Melissa whispered, trying not to feel disappointed. "I thought she might."

"I spoke to her this morning," Celeste rushed to explain. "She's still not feeling well."

"And she's still mad at me, isn't she?"

Celeste sighed. "Every time I bring up your name, she changes the subject. I'm trying my best, Melissa, but it's not easy."

"I know," Melissa said. "Maybe I should stop by her house on my way home. Maybe if I tried talking with her myself, it would help."

"You can't do that!" Celeste scolded. "You have to get ready for the dance."

"Izzy's more important than the dance."

"I know, but tonight's your night, Melissa.

If you stop by her house, you know you're going to get into a fight. Don't let her spoil things for you."

"You're right," Melissa reluctantly admitted. "Maybe she needs some more time to cool off."

"Hey, Melissa!" Seth cried. "The football team's throwing a victory party before the dance. Want to go?"

"I'll see you later," Celeste said, walking away.

"Celeste! Wait!" Melissa called as she watched her retreating back. "Don't go! Come with us."

Celeste turned around, walking backward. "Thanks for the invite, but I wouldn't fit in. You go have fun with your new friends. I'll see you at the dance tonight."

Melissa started to go after Celeste, but Seth grabbed her by the arm. "Come on, Melissa. Everyone's waiting."

The victory party lasted for two hours. Melissa had a good time, but by the time she got home, there was only an hour to get ready for the dance. Luckily all she had to do was change into her dress and freshen her makeup. Because Seth's car was in the garage getting a new set of shocks, Melissa was going to meet him at the dance.

The house was quiet when Melissa arrived home. Her parents had already left for their weekend trip, but Salt and Pepper weren't anywhere around, which she found strange. Usually they came running whenever they heard the front door open.

She called out to them a few times and even shook a box of dry cat food, but they still didn't appear. Maybe they were sleeping.

Once upstairs in her bedroom, Melissa freshened up the blush on her cheeks and added a dab of lip gloss. She also gave herself a spritz of perfume. Then she went to her closet to take out her dress to make sure it wasn't wrinkled. If it was, she'd give it a fast pressing.

Melissa opened her closet door. When she saw what was hanging inside, she gasped, taking a step back.

She clasped a hand over her open mouth, unable to believe what she was seeing.

"No!" she wailed. "No!"

Chapter 20

Her dress for the Homecoming dance had been slashed. It hung from its hanger in tattered strips, ruined beyond repair.

Melissa started to reach for the hanger with a trembling hand, but then slammed the closet door shut. She couldn't bring herself to touch the dress. She didn't even want to look at it.

Whoever slashed the dress had attacked it in a savage frenzy.

It must have happened this afternoon during the Homecoming ceremony. When she'd left the house after lunch with her parents, the dress had been fine.

Who could have done such a horrible thing? Was it Zach? Izzy? Laurel? Who hated her so much?

An even more frightening thought slithered into Melissa's mind just then, chilling her blood.

Whoever slashed the dress had been able to get into her house.

Could that person still be inside?

Melissa spun around, expecting to find herself facing a knife-wielding maniac. Her eyes darted around her bedroom, looking for the slightest movement, but all was still.

For now.

Suddenly, Melissa felt trapped. All she wanted to do was get outside, but what if someone was still in the house? She was on the second floor. In order to get down to the first floor, she'd have to head back out into the hallway past the guest room and her parents' bedroom.

What if someone was waiting to jump out from behind one of the half-open doors?

If only she'd left her cordless phone in her room, she could have called for help.

Melissa opened her bedroom door, warily sticking her head out. She listened, trying to make out the slightest sound, but all was silent.

Melissa took a tentative step out into the hallway. As she did, she heard the sound of a creak.

Her eyes darted across the hall and she gasped.

The door to the guest bedroom was starting to open!

Melissa tried to run, but was paralyzed, too scared to move.

She expected someone to come lunging out at her. Instead, the door stopped moving. A second later Salt and Pepper came bounding out of the guest room. They meowed at Melissa and then hurried down the stairs.

Watching Salt and Pepper disappear, Melissa leaned against her bedroom door, her body sagging with relief.

Without giving herself a chance to change her mind, she ran down the hallway. Bounding down the stairs, she expected to hear footsteps thundering behind her, but there weren't any.

Once downstairs she ran into the living room for her cordless phone. After snatching it up, she ran outside to her car and called the police, asking to speak with Detective Caruso. He wasn't in, so Melissa left a message. The second she hung up, the phone rang.

"Hello?"

"Hi, it's me," Celeste said. "I was calling to see how you were doing. What's wrong? You sound funny."

"Something happened," Melissa began, pouring out her story.

"That's terrible," Celeste gasped when Melissa had finished. "What are you going to wear to the dance?"

"I don't know." Melissa looked at her watch. "The mall's about to close, so I can't buy anything new. And I'm too scared to go back inside until the police check things out. At least I still have my robe and crown. I left them in my car before going inside. I guess I'm stuck with what I'm wearing."

"Oh no, you're not," Celeste stated firmly. "I bought a new dress to wear to my cousin Maria's wedding next month. You can wear that. Why don't I meet you at school in the girls' locker room and you can change there?"

Melissa's spirits lifted. "Celeste, you're a lifesaver. I don't know what I'd do without you."

"I'll see you in a little bit," Celeste said.

After shutting off the phone, Melissa pulled out of her driveway and drove to Westdale High. When she got there, the student parking lot was deserted and the hallways empty. On her way to the girls' locker room, she stopped in the gym, which was decorated with brightly colored streamers and balloons for the dance.

A romantic grotto with trees and a goldfish pond had also been created. The goldfish pond was actually a three-foot-deep pool surrounded by plastic boulders and rocks. The potted trees were strung with twinkling white lights and had rustic benches situated in front of them. Other twinkling white lights had been strung from one end of the gym to the other and two bright spotlights were situated over the Homecoming king and queen's thrones.

As Melissa walked through the gym, she was careful to avoid the cords and extensions that led to an elaborate electrical circuit system which would control the lights and music.

No one was around. There weren't even any teachers. It looked like she and Celeste were the only ones there so far.

Carrying her robe, crown, and scepter under one arm, Melissa hurried to the girls' locker room, where she found Celeste waiting. She was already dressed for the dance, looking terrific in a midnight blue dress. Her hair wasn't in its usual ponytail and she was even wearing some makeup.

"You don't know how much I appreciate this," Melissa said when Celeste handed her a white box.

"We can't have a Homecoming queen who doesn't look like a queen," Celeste said, relieving Melissa of her robe, crown, and scepter. "I'll hold these until you're dressed."

"Thanks."

Melissa was speechless when she lifted the lid off the box and saw the dress inside — it was beautiful. It was white, with a scooped neckline, made of a lacelike material. It looked so fragile, she was almost afraid to take it out of the box.

"It's gorgeous," Melissa whispered. "There's something really old-fashioned about it. Has Izzy seen it? She's going to flip."

"No one's seen it but you," Celeste said, helping Melissa slip into the dress. "Do you really like it?"

"I love it," Melissa raved, admiring herself in a full-length mirror against the wall.

"Promise you'll be careful with it," Celeste said.

"You know I will."

"Promise!" Celeste snapped, a sharp tone in her voice.

Melissa turned away from the mirror. "I promise," she said. "What's wrong?"

"I'm sorry. It's just that the dress means a lot to me."

"How come?"

"It belonged to my aunt."

"Your aunt?" Melissa looked at Celeste in confusion. "I thought you said you bought it for your cousin Maria's wedding next month."

Celeste shook her head. "You must have misheard me."

"I could have sworn you said you bought it."

"I didn't," Celeste insisted.

"My mistake," Melissa said, turning back to the mirror, although she was *sure* she was right. But why would Celeste lie? "Which aunt did it belong to? Have I ever met her?"

"No," Celeste answered. "You've never met her. I've never even met her."

"What do you mean?"

"She's dead," Celeste said.

"Dead?"

"She died very young. Very tragically. She was only seventeen."

"How awful," Melissa said.

"That dress was her graduation dress," Celeste said. "She was supposed to have been valedictorian of her class. She had a full scholarship to an Ivy League college and she dreamed of becoming a doctor. She was the smartest and prettiest girl at Westdale High."

"She went to Westdale High?" Melissa asked. "What was her name?"

"*Brenda*," Celeste whispered.

Hearing the name of Celeste's aunt, Melissa's heart nearly stopped. Warning bells went off in her head, but she ignored them. It had to be a coincidence. That's all it was. A coincidence. Brenda Sheldon couldn't be Celeste's aunt.

"How did she die?" Melissa asked.

"It was a car accident," Celeste said softly. "It happened the night she was crowned Homecoming queen."

A feeling of unease crept over Melissa. "Your aunt was Brenda Sheldon?" she whispered over the lump in her throat.

"That's right," Celeste answered. "She was."

Suddenly nervous about being alone with Celeste, Melissa turned around. When she did, she was shocked to see Celeste wearing her Homecoming crown and robe.

Even more shocking was the knife in her hand.

"You?" Melissa whispered in disbelief. "It was you all along?"

"Yes," Celeste hissed, moving closer and raising the knife in her hand. "It was me."

"But why?"

"Why not?" Celeste demanded, her voice rising. "After what happened to my aunt, Westdale High should never have had another Homecoming queen."

"Why didn't you ever say anything?" Melissa asked.

"Why? Would it have made a difference? After my aunt died, everyone forgot about her. They turned her into a joke! A ghost story! Everyone in Westdale laughed at her."

Celeste drew closer to Melissa, tightening the grip on her knife. "You don't deserve to be Homecoming queen," she raged, her body shaking with fury. "You don't deserve to wear this crown. None of you do! When I heard Westdale High was going to have another Homecoming queen, I decided to make sure you would all pay!"

"You were the one behind everything?" Melissa asked. "It was never anyone else?"

Celeste nodded her head gleefully. "That's right. Sweet innocent Celeste. No one would ever suspect me. *I* was the one who dropped that sandbag. *I* was the one who sent you those dead flowers and made those phone calls. *I* was the 'ghost' you saw the night you left the library. It was never Laurel or Betsy or Zach or Izzy. It was always me."

Melissa couldn't believe what she was hearing. Celeste was the one who had been terrorizing her all these weeks.

"At first I just wanted to scare you so you'd

drop out of the running," Celeste explained. "You were my friend, Melissa. I didn't want to hurt you. But you wouldn't drop out. And then you became friends with Faith and Tia. That was your big mistake."

"Why?"

"You betrayed our friendship. You lied to me!" Celeste screeched, her face transforming into a mask of hatred. "I saw you that night at the library with Faith and Tia. You said you couldn't come over to my house because you had a paper to write, but when I went to the library, I saw you with them."

"I didn't lie," Melissa said. "I went to the library to work on my paper and I ran into them."

"I hated Faith and Tia even more after that night," Celeste spat, ignoring Melissa's words. "So I decided they should suffer." Celeste's eyes glinted insanely. "And I decided you should die."

Celeste moved forward and Melissa instinctively took a step back. Her mind was reeling and she forced herself to concentrate. With Celeste in her path, backing her into a corner and blocking her way with the knife she held, there was no way for her to escape. The best thing she could do was keep her talking.

Hopefully students would start arriving for the dance. Once she heard someone, she could scream for help.

"Tell me about your aunt Brenda," Melissa said. "What was she like?"

At the mention of her aunt, a smile washed over Celeste's face and she lowered her hand holding the knife. "My aunt was sweet and kind and good. She was my mother's baby sister. My mother and her family were devastated after she died and they moved away. It was too painful living in Westdale, but that didn't compare to the pain when we moved back."

"Why?" Melissa asked.

"No one remembered my mother or that she was Brenda Sheldon's sister," Celeste explained. "But worse than that, no one remembered Aunt Brenda. By then, she'd been turned into a horrible legend. It made me so mad! As far back as I can remember, my mother always told me about my aunt Brenda. She told me how smart and pretty she was. How I had to grow up to be just like her and make everyone proud."

Celeste admired herself in the mirror. "Did you know I resemble my aunt Brenda? Everyone in my family says so. If anyone should be Homecoming queen, it should be me."

Celeste laughed harshly and the smile on her face disappeared. "Can you believe they're having Homecoming weekend in memory of Betsy? What about my aunt? She's the one who should be remembered. Not Betsy!"

"Why did you kill Betsy?" Melissa asked.

"She deserved more than an accident," Celeste hissed. "She was always making fun of other people. I hate people like that. People like that deserve to die."

"How did you know she'd be at the Laundromat?"

"I didn't. I found out when I followed you that night. When I got to the Laundromat, I watched through the window and saw Betsy and Laurel pull their trick on you. After you left, Laurel and Betsy stayed behind to wash Betsy's jacket. When Laurel finally left, I went inside and killed Betsy."

"Why did you want me to think Izzy was the killer?"

Celeste laughed hysterically. "It was so easy! Anything I told you, you believed. Like that newspaper clipping. It didn't fall out of her notebook — I only said it did and you didn't doubt me."

"I believed you because I trusted you. I thought you were my friend," Melissa said angrily. "You told me you thought Izzy might be the killer. I believed you and that destroyed my friendship with her."

"You didn't deserve Izzy's friendship!" Celeste shouted. "You forgot all about us once you were nominated for Homecoming queen. You became just like Laurel and Betsy."

"That's not true!"

"Yes, it is! We were good enough for you last semester, but this semester you didn't need us anymore. You were too busy with your new friends!"

"No, I wasn't," Melissa cried. "You and Izzy are my best friends."

"Liar!" Celeste spat out. "You'll say anything to save yourself."

"I'm not lying! I'm telling you the truth."

"So am I," Celeste whispered, closing the distance between them, the grip on her knife tightening. "I hate you, Melissa. When I slashed your dress I pretended you were wearing it. I pretended my knife was digging into your skin, slashing your flesh to ribbons the way I slashed that dress to shreds."

"Celeste, please," Melissa begged. "You can't do this."

"But I have to," Celeste said. "Don't you understand? I have to do it for Aunt Brenda."

"But your aunt is dead!" Melissa cried. "She's dead!"

Celeste shook her head. "It doesn't matter. I have to make things right for her. She has to have her revenge."

"You'll never get away with it."

"Oh, won't I?" Celeste laughed. "No one would *ever* suspect me. I'll never get caught. I'm too smart, Melissa. Haven't you realized that?"

Melissa shrank back from Celeste in fear, her eyes never leaving the knife that was coming closer and closer. She could almost see her reflection in the knife's broad blade.

"I'm not going to mess up this time," Celeste promised, raising the knife over her head. "This time you're going to die!"

"Izzy!" Melissa screamed, eyes widening as she stared over Celeste's shoulder. "What are you doing here? Run! She's got a knife."

Celeste whirled around and Melissa seized the moment. She'd fallen for her bluff! She pushed Celeste to the ground and ran for the nearest exit. As she did, she grabbed her scepter off the floor. If Celeste came after her, she needed something to defend herself with.

"You won't get away!" Celeste shrieked. "I'll find you. And when I do, you're dead!"

Melissa ran as fast as she could in her high heels. She didn't dare look over her shoulder.

She was afraid if she saw Celeste behind her, she'd freeze.

Melissa hurried back up to the first floor. When she reached the top of the stairs, she ran for the nearest exit. She pushed against the steel-gray door, expecting it to open, but it didn't.

"Come on," Melissa begged, shoving against the door with all her might. She looked nervously over her shoulder, listening for Celeste. "Open!"

She tried again and again, but it was no use. The door was locked. Behind her she could hear Celeste's footsteps coming up the stairs. She didn't have time to make it to the other end of the hallway. She had no choice but to run to the gym.

The gym was still empty when Melissa arrived. She hurried underneath the bleachers, clutching her scepter.

Almost immediately, she heard footsteps, followed by the sound of the gym doors slamming open.

"Come out, come out wherever you are," Celeste called in a sing-song voice.

From between the slats of the bleachers, Melissa could see Celeste walk by. As she watched, she tried not to make a sound. Celeste then disappeared from sight and she heard her going from one end of the gym to the other. After that she heard the gym doors slam against the hall walls as Celeste stormed out.

And then there was silence.

Even though Celeste was gone, Melissa stayed hidden, fearful of her return. Finally, when she felt it was safe, she stepped out from underneath the bleachers.

When she did, she heard a voice.

"That was stupid."

Melissa looked up. Sitting in the middle of the bleachers, quiet as a mouse, was Celeste. Knife raised high, her face twisted with fury, she sprang out of her seat and lunged at Melissa. As Celeste descended upon her, Melissa raised her scepter and used it to knock Celeste's knife out of her hand. It flew across the gym, clattering to the floor.

Celeste landed on top of Melissa with a heavy thump, knocking her down. Melissa's scepter fell out of her hand, rolling far from her reach. As Celeste lay motionless on top of her, Melissa shoved her off and struggled to get to her feet, trying to run for the exit. But before she could get very far, Celeste tackled her from behind, knocking her back to the floor.

"You're not going anywhere!" Celeste screeched.

Melissa spun around, kicking out at Celeste as she jumped up. She looked around desperately for her lost scepter, but couldn't find it.

"Looking for this?" Celeste asked, raising the scepter in one hand.

Melissa began backing away from Celeste as she closed in with the scepter, swinging it back and forth. By this point their struggle had reached the goldfish pond, while the white lights in the trees around them winked on and off.

Melissa tried to zigzag out of Celeste's aim, but wasn't fast enough. The scepter smashed into her arm, and Melissa fell to the floor. A dull, throbbing pain shot up her arm. It was the moment Celeste had been waiting for.

"It's time to die, Melissa," she whispered softly. "It's time to die."

As Celeste moved in for the kill, Melissa summoned up the last of her strength. Using both feet, she shoved Celeste away from her as she charged.

Melissa's feet connected with Celeste's stomach and the strength of her shove caused Celeste, still clutching the metal scepter, to crash against the side of the goldfish pond. Trying to maintain her balance, Celeste's arms wrapped around one of the trees strung with twinkling white lights.

But instead of regaining her balance, Celeste fell backward into the water.

Instantly, there was a flash of bright sparks, and Melissa could hear Celeste's anguished moans, the loud sizzle of burning flesh. After a burst of flames, there was the sound of Celeste's last, agonized screams as she was electrocuted.

Epilogue

"Is the scary part over yet?" Melissa asked, peeking through her fingers at the television.

"It's over," Izzy said.

Melissa lowered her fingers just as the movie's hockey-masked killer crashed through a living-room window. "Izzy!" she exclaimed, jumping in her seat.

"You call that scary?" Izzy said, reaching for a handful of popcorn from a bowl on the coffee table.

Melissa swatted her with a pillow. It was Halloween night and they were having an all-night horror movie marathon at Melissa's house. Things were back to the way they used to be and Melissa couldn't be happier. Of course, things weren't *exactly* the same. Celeste was gone.

"What's the matter?" Izzy asked. "You suddenly look sad."

"I was thinking of Celeste."

Izzy sighed. "Oh, Melissa. No one could have helped her. She listened to those stories her mother told her for so long. You read all the newspaper articles. She became obsessed with her aunt. There was nothing we could have done, Melissa."

"I know."

"Look at the way she lied to us," Izzy continued. "Instead of trying to help us patch up our friendship, she was feeding us both lies. She tried to make you think I was a killer and she tried to make me think you had betrayed me."

Just then Seth came into the living room with a pizza box. His cheeks were red from the cold October night and his hair was windblown. Trailing behind him were Salt and Pepper, lured by the tantalizing scent of pepperoni and anchovies.

"Did I miss much?" he asked, placing the pizza box on the coffee table.

"Just some talk," Melissa said, opening the box and passing a slice of pizza to Izzy. Then she passed one to Seth and settled on the couch next to him with her own slice.

"Have you got everything you need?" Seth asked, wrapping an arm around Melissa's shoulders.

Melissa looked around the living room. "Pizzas, sodas, munchies. My best friend and boyfriend." She snuggled closer to Seth. "I'd say I have everything I need. In fact, I'd say this is the best Halloween I've had in years!"

Point Horror

COLLECTIONS

Are you hooked on horror? Are you prepared to be scared? Then read on for three helpings of horror...

Point Horror
Specials

For Point Horror afficinados everywhere, three deluxe hardback editions from your favourite Point Horror authors...

1: The R.L. Stine Special
The Baby-sitter I, The Baby-sitter II, The Baby-sitter III

2: The Diane Hoh Special
The Fever, Funhouse, The Invitation

3: The Caroline B. Cooney Special
Freeze Tag, The Stranger, Twins

Point Horror

Dare you read

NIGHTMARE HALL

Where college is a
scream!

High on a hill overlooking Salem University hidden in shadows and shrouded in mystery, sits Nightingale Hall.

Nightmare Hall, the students call it. Because that's where the terror began...

Don't miss these spine-tingling thrillers: